# Reversal

Rocco Scibetta

ISBN 978-1-954345-94-2 (paperback)
ISBN 978-1-954345-96-6 (digital)



Rushmore Press LLC
1 800 460 9188
www.rushmorepress.com

Printed in the United States of America

# PART ONE

## SARAH DYLAN WELLES

Milan, Italy. Hotel Saint Angelo

With a gloved hand, inspector Salvino Proust pokes through the cooling embers of a spent fire. He scribbles a note, handing it off to another man with instructions on whom to send the findings to in New York, specifically the Bureau of Investigations.

Amongst the discarded ashes and partially burned remains, a slim volume of poems was retrieved from the fireplace. A page was bent and earmarked at the corner, oddly pinched and rubbed with a smudge of a greasy substance, possibly a hand cream or a cosmetic ointment. A full thumbprint was identified as that of Dylan Welles.

Salvino Proust was intrigued by the handwriting. He ran the parchment beneath his nose, sniffing the fragrance of an exotic substance that lifted from the page. A montage of images began to form in his mind from the many paparazzi photos and magazine interviews he was exposed to over time concerning the self-made diva D. Welles. The media exposure of Dylan Welles was part of a fantasy life as well as a legacy she left to thousands of readers throughout the art world.

Proust, a seasoned professional, always regarded evidence with the clear cold detachment of an investigative reporter; to deal only with facts was a hardwired mantra developed in his being. Fantasy was not something he involved himself with. The fleeting ether rising from this twisted page was, however, the last known scent of Dylan Welles. The fact was that he was holding a scant ephemeral part of her in his hand and a partial poem was handwritten, most likely by Dylan Welles, providing a glimpse into her private mind at a time when she might be most vulnerable. This stirred a deep excitement in him, almost fetish-like in its arousal. Dylan Welles, the bon vivant celebrity art dealer. Dylan Welles, femme fatal. Dylan Welles, infamous jet-set relationship with international bad-boy Franco Delacroix. Dylan Welles was found dead hanging from a scaffold in her New York Gallery—an apparent suicide.

> In the land of the father
> Our daily bread.
> A bundle of fine rags with matching shoes
> Bows her head.

He pondered the cryptic words and then scribbled on his notepad the following: all other furnishings and artifacts concerning the case were exactly as they should be.


## Inspector Salvino Proust, Milan

It was the year of her tenth birthday. It was a year that began with a fragile memory that locked itself in the mind of a young girl. As a young child, bearing the gift for remembering such things, she carried that year in her heart for the rest of her life. It began with winter that particular year. Winter became the spring; by the time the brownness of autumn came to be, death was already creeping in, slowly making its velleity known. The slight germ of a wish was not accompanied as of yet by any effort or action, or even a sinister thought as to how to entertain it.

This wish, ever so slight, was bestowed that year on a morose, young child fated to walk the glorious atrium of fame and terrible beauty.

Sarah Dylan Welles sat at her desk with her hands clasped nervously around the edge of her textbooks. She especially liked the thick history book that she always placed on top of the others not so much for its content, but more for the fabric veneer cover that frayed at the corner edges, exposing silky linen-like fibers tightly woven around a soft splintered cardboard pushing through. Sarah has a compulsion to fidget, rubbing soft materials such as silk labels and pinching fabrics between her thumb and forefingers. She would sometimes in her bed fold the cloth of the broad linen bed sheet in such a way that she could rub the cuticle of her index finger against the pointed cloth, causing a sensation of gentle calm and well-being. This was a euphoria she would never be able to explain throughout her life. It was a minor compulsion that may have manifested after being hospitalized for a childhood illness when she was four, an experience she can feel more than remember. This déjà vu disorientation became a familiar experience to her, stemming from a melancholy place in her psychic memory.

Her Aunt Caroline, overprotective, mothering Aunt Caroline, would visit her at the hospital. On one occasion, she brought a cloth doll that Sarah attached herself to, sort of a surrogate "Auntie" for lack of a better term. It became a comfort to her after visitor hours ended.

Being only a very young child confused by illness and fever, the primary emotions Sarah was to be saddened with were love, longing, and abandonment.

Sarah grew into a tall lanky fourth-grader, graceful like a cat, and never clumsy or awkward. She could be and was pretty, very pretty. However, the first impression most people experienced right off was that of a gothic malaise, a disquiet that emanated from her dark linen hair and large absorbing eyes. Her hair was especially captivating. They were flaxen strands laid one upon another in a heaping design like the polyester assembly of a doll wig. So dark was her hair that glimpses of Persian blue would radiate. And then the eyes, those extraordinary eyes, huge like plump olives and just the same dull umber hue are large enough to see the world in all directions, while lackluster enough not to lend her feelings any description at all, a trait that would serve her well throughout her life. She was a pale child. Her skin was so thin and translucent at the temples that sometimes Aunt Caroline could see the blue of her veins pulsing as she slept. Caroline recalls Sarah's father possessing the same rhythmic throbbing characteristic as he slept on those teenage slumber binges below the pier.

It was Friday afternoon in the classroom; Sarah is absorbed through a crack in the corner wall by the great window. She is daydreaming again.

Outside, the streets were crowding with parents who showed up every day at the same time to pick up their children.

Caroline stood faithfully on the same corner, patient as always, just below the large window, arms folded or sometimes hands pushed into the pockets of her long gray coat.

Sarah shifted her enormous eyes on Mrs. Ranshak, the homeroom teacher. Sarah observed her large scary head and exaggerated features. How different she was from the other women Sarah had been exposed to in her small town.

Mrs. Ranshak's clothes were always crisp and tailored. Her skirts and jackets were distinct colors, and her shoes caused a monotonous thud when she walked across the planked wooden floor.

At night sometimes, Sarah would lie in bed and think about Mrs. Ranshak's face: her thick butternut complexion with red frightening lips that pull forward when she stressed a point or gnawed her gum, exposing a softer pink rim around the edges of her mouth. The thin film of saliva that coated her teeth, adding an artificial gleam to what otherwise would be dull yellow enamel—"The color that people's fingertips turn when they smoke too many cigarettes," Sara noted to herself.

Mrs. Ranshak was a smoker. She could consume about eight to twelve Pall Malls a day. As a consequence of her vice, she was constantly chewing gum, causing her jaw to swing in a left to right semi-circular motion, appearing almost unhinged at times folding her bottom lip back over her teeth with each rotation. Sarah shifted her eyes again to a book on her schoolmate's desk. It was their fourth-grade reader. The cover depicted two children, a boy, and a girl accompanied by a postman and a dog. The characters were like herself, she thought, but not the same in a cartoon sense, very much not the same.

From where her desk was positioned, if Sarah stood up, she could see Auntie waiting outside; however, being scolded on numerous occasions for leaving her seat, she knew to sit still or suffer public humiliation. Restraining to fidget, she went back to rubbing her cuticle against the edge of the book cover.

Sarah thought to herself, "What if the teacher becomes horribly angry and would not let us leave our seats for a very long time, a very long time after the bell had rung?" Sarah looked toward the window and wondered if Aunt Caroline was waiting for her. Sarah imagined her Auntie waiting silently, with her arms folded across her chest, holding down a frock of her hair against the wind. Would she wait? How long? Would she eventually go home and not know when to come back? (fidget, fidget, fidget)

The bell rang, snapping Sarah and the others out of their somnambulant trances.

"Keep in line! No shoving on the stairs," the teacher warned. Sarah, not wanting to look up, walked past the teacher, through the door, did not shove in the stairwell, walked on to the street, and ran into her Auntie's arms.

The voice on the radio would not stop talking about it. Every tabloid had it printed boldly across its newspaper skin, most reports, and current media kept you up to date with the latest doppler radar updates on its movement. The storm was being heralded as the trendiest weather occurrence of the decade.

It was talked about like the most spoiled celebrity in Hollywood, described with all the dangerous bad boy elements of a naughty rock star. It was given a sexy name: Deirdre. It originated off the coast of the Caribbean Gulfstream and developed from its humble origins as a small tropical storm to a major hurricane in just a few days. Deirdre grabbed the attention of everyone from weather reporters wearing fashionable rain gear, to tourists caught in the worst vacation of their lives. Deirdre twisted palm trees and collapsed shanty villages as easily as one yawn. Palace hotels were boarded up, and vacationers were being videotaped evacuating in a mass exodus through one-lane highways, leaving the sandy beaches in the hands of a domineering mother tempest. Courageous news of people hoping to make their bones tied themselves to steel railings as they described the windstorm fury before them.

Deirdre will soon merge with other storm systems, gathering enough momentum to travel up the coast in a few days with enough force to unleash its havoc on a neighboring beach near you.

"Not since 1929 has any storm been this dangerous. At the turn of the century, Cuba and Key west almost blew into each other," one reporter remembers. "Only a few can recall recent nor'easters such as this." CPF NEWS Florida has an exclusive interview. "John Wild was there as a young man fishing off the mangroves when the first squalls of our most recent hurricane, Jocelyn, rattled his small boat. Today, he is blind, crippled, and crazy, but he will always remember those menacing clouds pounding the Keys with buckets of rain with winds up to 165 miles per hour."

Saturday was the county antique fair. There were about 48 good hours before the storm began blustering its way into Sarah's hometown of Barn Hope, Maryland. Caroline and her Mother were not originally from Barn Hope, but they moved there nine years prior when Sara was born. Sarah never knew her mother or her father; there were always just Auntie Caroline and Grandma.

Caroline was a spinster type of woman of twenty–seven, pretty and a little stocky. She shared with Sarah her family dark hair and eyes, but not her facial structure and coloring. Caroline was rubicund with chiseled cheekbones and a prominent forehead that gave the impression of a receding hairline. She ran a small curiosity shop that her mother helped her with, and together, they did quite well. The building was large enough to convert to living quarters so all three of them could function comfortably and independently under one roof. Learning the different styles and period pieces of furniture and folk art was interesting, and everyone stayed occupied, especially Sarah who absorbed everything like a sponge.

Sarah had a gifted eye for things of quality; at nine years old, she was an asset to Caroline on her antique runs to flea markets and estate sales, rummaging through waste piles and curiosity items.

On this day, Sarah brought back from the fair a whimsical item. She waited with propensity all morning to get to a certain vendor she always frequented on her visits. The vendor was selling a broken darning basket with some odd sewing accessories and darning needles. The going price was five dollars. His table was mostly rusty cellar items such as tools, molded books, garden accessories, and a few old picture frames.

Every fair has a local eccentric; "Silver Bells," as he is known to local fossickers, belongs to Barn Hope. He is a peculiar old chap dressed in work overalls and a military coat adorned with pins of all kinds, with a long gray ponytail that has silver bells dangling from it. The silver bells gently ringing became the conspicuous item of attention. His oddness was kept in check by a long unkempt beard.

Sarah was always felt drawn to his table, immediately attracted to the unconventional behavior of it all. Even at the early age of nine, she was lured by different and creative people and intuitive magnetism that stayed with her all her life.

After raiding her savings jar of five dollars, she was able to bargain old Silver Bells down to three dollars for the basket and all of its contents. When presented to her Aunt and Grandma, however, no one was pleased.

"Sarah, you spent that money you saved so hard to buy this crap! I am not angry that you tried to do well. I am disappointed because I thought you knew better than to throw money away like that. And that Silver Bells, just wait till I get a hold of him, taking advantage..." With a heaving sigh, Caroline gave in. "Oh well, let's see what you found."

Sarah lifted the basket to the table with a huff and removed some items from it. Caroline and Grandma looked on with unenthusiastic faces, passing glances back and forth, looking over some rusted darning needles and a useless barb with thread.

Sarah reached in and pulled out a small leather packet; removing a thimble, she held it out in the palm of her hand. "I had to buy the broken basket to get this. Look!" she exclaimed. "This is the same kind of thimble that I saw in that book on the bookshelf." Presented to Caroline was a Royale Doubleton porcelain thimble with a painted base and a tiny gold inscription carefully encrypted with a date year of seventeen seventy-eight. The porcelain when held up to the light was flawlessly perfect.

"My God, Sarah, how did you notice this? I walked past the junk table for weeks, and I never saw it," Caroline said.

"I just looked inside the basket, and there it was in this brown little case," Sarah responded.

"Well, young lady, you just turned your three-dollar investment into, I'm thinking, maybe two hundred dollars."

It was during that year that Sarah celebrated her last happy birthday. There was a birthday cake with ten candles on it, some lovely presents, and new clothes. The most thrilling thing was a trip to the grown-ups' beauty parlor for the first time. It was special for Sarah that year, feeling excited as a young girl would whose age years now jumped into the two-digit numerals, bringing her that much closer to a teenager. Added was the arrival of an early menstrual cycle initiating her into untimely womanhood.

The storm of the millennium came and went, bringing some damage to Welles's home. With it followed in the aftermath the procession of handymen and drifters seeking odd jobs and daily work to get them enough cash to move on to their next location. A curious assortment of vagrant types cluttered the roads and byways. Some were fleeing the law, some down on their luck, and others were just free spirits making their way. It was during this year that a tall, pale, dark-haired man came to their door. Auntie was in recovery from an illness that seemed to be getting worse. The man hung around fixing things and bringing everything back to normal. It seemed they all knew each other pretty well—Auntie, Grandma, and this stranger. But Sarah was kept away and never introduced. The man came around in the morning, did his work, and left before Sarah came home from school. Sometimes, he would sleep in the large shed behind the house. When Auntie Caroline died many months later, it was the day of reckoning. After Auntie was buried, Grandma had some words with the man and he never came back. Grandma took Sarah alone one day and sat her down. She told her, "In a few years, Sarah, you will be an adult, and you will have to make your way. I may not be there for you. My health, as you may have noticed, is not that good and I am getting old. However, there are some things you should know. It was because of my daughter's wishes I have stayed silent; now that she has passed, it is only decent that you should know your history. That man that was doing work for us, did you get a good look at him?"

"Yes, Grandma."

"Remember him, Sarah. He is your father. He is an untrustworthy near-do-well who abandoned you and your mother when she became pregnant; she was a little more than the age you are now. In those days, it was a great scandal to have become an unwed mother so young. So, we all had to move and start again. Your mother always had a soft spot for him; she was a little more than a child when she was corrupted and never grew out of the game they played. If not for me, she would take him back and believe his lies. Life would be very hard and wrought with disappointment with a man like that, but that's all over now."

"Grandma, where is my mother? How come I never met her?"

"Child, your mother was your Auntie Caroline."


Nicolette, Vincent, and Tramp


Behind the cover of shady Catawba and sycamores, the ruddy brick façade of the Fennimore Stuart Art Building looms over the grounds like a grand old lion. A gust of wind kicks up dust twirling leaves of crimson maple, thwarting a cat in his attempts to skedaddle across the lawn.

Lifting a paw to his eye, he stops short to wipe a grain of dust away. The mysterious calico cat that romps these grounds is a familiar visitor amongst the locals. The feral friend makes his rounds in the wee hours. He makes a feast of his loyal patrons, snatching their goodies then going on his merry way. His transient behavior and sovereign lifestyle earned him the neighborhood name, "Tramp."

Calico cats are not a breed but a textured color pattern that can become the coat for many different animals. Tramp, as he is to be called, is most definitely a male. It is rare for a calico to be of the male gender. This is primarily because many of them have a condition known as Klinefelter syndrome, which causes them to carry two X chromosomes in addition to one Y chromosome. This leads directly to the distinctive coat coloring. Tramp is predominately white, with orange tiger-like patches over his left eye and half his back. The orange gene bringing him his wood fire glow can be traced back to the Mediterranean regions. His eyes are green.

If Tramp was a human, he would most likely be a loner, a prince in exile, content to rule his domain one small victory at a time. He might be a noir detective or a clever reporter. An ancient soul provides him with a love for music that he demonstrates by perching himself under the rafters outside the music rooms of Fennimore Symphonic Hall where the concert students rehearse. The round warm tones of the cellos soothe, avoiding the cooler pitches of the violin player's diatonic scales that sometimes hurt his ears. Piano relaxes, but only sonatas. In the spring, he explores the neighborhood gardens making a theater seat in Mrs. Cornwall's garden, watching the birds work and play. He is the perfect gentleman, never chasing them or harassing them in any way. At times, when a bullying squirrel becomes too overbearing, frightening the birds from their feeders and disrupting the play, Tramp is to the rescue; he would intervene chasing the predator away.

The king at court in the summer is a welcome visitor to the butchers and grocers. In the eastern quarter by the bayside, he chases mice and various harbor varmints from the dumpsters. In return, he is provided a cool nesting place close to the refrigeration units. Autumn and winter bring out the consummate busybody. From tenement fire escapes and brownstone ledges, Tramp pokes the kitchen screens and window shades, watching folks act out the drama of their daily lives. Only old man Rebus hates having him around.

Fitzgerald Rebus is a stodgy old character, a curmudgeon by day, and by night, the stereotypical shoe thrower constantly vigilant at his sentinel window, hurling empty cans of spent beans and old rolled-up socks at the feline choir howling at the moon.

It is a beautiful Saturday. It is a picturesque cityscape of umbrellas opening and closing as the smell of diners and pancake houses tempt patrons with greasy spoon enticements. Billboards with menus and early bird specials crowd the sidewalks. Summer is breaking up. The cool damp night drenched the leaves with tears, causing many to drop loose from their branches. A breeze lifted them just enough to swirl into a pile of circling dust and debris outside the door of a local art gallery. Two voices blend, causing an inaudible hum. In the window, art from various painters is on display. Broad strokes and color fields fill the venue adding to urban enchantment. Pedestrians come and go on route to conduct their business.

On the opposite corner, a man is dressed in a theatrical uniform handing out leaflets. As he attempts to separate pages, one escapes from his hand and blows along the street. It too finds its way to a pile of leaves churning up and around the gallery. Lying face-up, it reads, "Ava Dance Musical of the Year. All-Star Cast and New Debutant Stars."

It is late morning.

Vincent Galle is standing over the sink in his apartment watering his basil plants. After draining the herbs, he brings them to the fire escape and places them with the other plants to catch the sun. A lazy calico cat watches Vince perform his chores.

From his apartment window, Vincent could see Nicolette crossing Fourth Avenue with a bag in hand. He silently observes the strength in her gallop as she crosses against the traffic; this is something he admonishes her not to do, but Nicco, as Vince has come to accept, will yes you to death, and cross any damn way she pleases if it is more expedient. Vince shakes his head and sighs as a blue BMW zips around her, popping its horn in irritation. She looks up at the window and waved at Vince, not paying any regard whatsoever to the traffic pattern.

"It's a miracle," Vince mumbles to Tramp, "she is not a statistic by now."

Vince leans out the window and waves back, pointing at his watch.

"I know, I know," she calls back. Nicco cups a hand to her mouth and calls to Vince, "Throw me a line!"

Vince partially leans out the window tying a rope around the handle of a wide basket; he lowers it down onto the street.

Nicco catches the basket, putting the bag into it. She signals Vince to haul it back up. Nicco blows him a kiss and hurries off down the street.

Vince pulls the basket back up and unloads it, bringing the bag inside and placing it gently on the counter space. He removes a quart of milk from the bag along with some eggs and cookies. No matter how short on cash they are, Nicco always drums up enough spare change to surprise Vince with a Linzer tart from the bakery. On the side of the bag, there is writing, "Off to rehearsal. Don't forget to feed Tramp. See ya later. Luv ya lots, Nicci."

Vince goes into the refrigerator and opens a foil packet containing a small piece of salmon, and he mashes it with a fork. Pouring some milk into a bowl, he places them outside for Tramp who was already watching from the crow's nest. Tramp stealthily gets his footing then leaps to the iron grill slats of the near century-old fire escape.

"Dance! When you're broken open, dance! If you've torn the bandage off, dance! In the middle of the fighting, dance! In your blood, dance! When you're perfectly free..."

The Buzz-Beat Dance Studio is a red brick-and-mortar splendor smack in the middle of Jones Street, the most exciting place to be if you are a dancer with promise.

At 362 Jones Street sits a converted factory that now houses four huge floors of dance and film experiences. At any time, you could see film crews going up and down the elevators, interviewing future divas, or promoting important new stage productions. Famous singers and dancers from as far as Russia and Europe use the facility to rehearse when they are in town. On these special occasions, one whole floor is closed just for their exclusive convenience. From Nicco's studio window, the members from the Ava Dance Troupe watch the limos escort divas in and out from the humble parking lot in the back to their world-renowned avant-garde accommodations. To be a part of that privileged information is awe-inspiring.

The rooms where the Ava Dance Troupe rehearses are state-of-the-art. The floors are polished wood with long mirrors that covered the walls from floor to ceiling. The ceiling is original plaster and moldings with huge fans that hang quarter ways down.

A thick wooden dowel extended across the length of the room. Nicci hoisted her leg over the bar and stretched, holding her ankle in place slowly touching her head to her knee. Soft music pumped in from the speakers, causing her to flow and dip in rhythm. Five days a week, she practiced alone for the first twenty minutes of her workout before joining the others for her scheduled rehearsal. This was her preferred routine. Today, however, slight anxiety distracted her from the full focus she normally generates.

She hesitated for a moment, noticing herself in the mirror. Her elongated body was fit and lean snugly compressed in a cotton leotard. Turning sideways, she ran her hand along her stomach, her face in the mirror reflects her eyes slowly following her hand along the abdomen, studying it for any bulges. She sighed and walked over to a scale at the end of the studio and stepped on.

The busy hallways were a buzz for dancers walking in and out of rooms checking for privacy; most of the dancers kept to themselves focusing on their dance parts. There was little time for the interruption. Nic's good friend Ozzie wandered by just in time to catch Nicci at the inopportune moment of cursing at the scale. Ozzie approaches with the look of intuitive curiosity.

"Nic, how long you been here?"

"Ozzie!"

Nicci acknowledged a little shaken, not stirred. "You woke me up. I was daydreaming. I just got in a little while ago. I'm running late today. I had a doctor's appointment at one o'clock." Nicco held back her tongue, and she quickly realized her slip; she should not have blurted out anything about a doctor.

Ozzie noticed a despondent look. "Hey, everything ok?"

"Yeah, you know routine stuff. B12 shot, all that."

Ozzie went on, "Hey Nic, I have some good news. You weren't here this morning. I am being considered for that part in the Ava Dance Troupe. I just got word from the head man himself."

Nicci gets excited and jumps in jubilation. "We are going to be sharing the same stage, girl! I am so happy for you. This is just what we hoped for."

They both begin jumping up and down high fiving each other.

"It's looking good." Hugs and fist bumps followed by more elation.

"You believe it! This is our first real break."

Ozzie gets solemn, pulling Nicci in front of her. The mist of genuine sentiment was welling up in Ozzie's eyes.

"Nic, I have to thank you. If not for your coaching, I could not have done this. I'll never forget it. I owe you big time, sis."

"You're my best friend, Ozz. That's the way we roll." They high five once more and laugh it off.

Ozzie questions, "What's with the scale thing? When I came in, you were staring at it like it was one of those fortune-telling machines at the arcade."

"I have been late-night binging with Vince. Doesn't it show? I mean, I need to stop snacking."

Ozzie replies, "Maybe just a tad around the middle, but you can knock that off quickly."

"You bet." The optimistic smile drops from Nicco's face as a look of worry replaces it in the mirror. Ozzie turned away as she lowered her bag; she never noticed the worried look in Nicci's eyes.

—Early evening rush hour.

The hamburger crowd is gathering around the corners of Jones and Harlequin Street. Its controlled chaos is always on schedule, same time, and same railway station, rain or shine.

The usual suspects crowd the pavement and taxis hustle to get that long-haul fare. Preppy young men unchain their bicycles from the stands, taking a moment to adjust their absurd safety helmets. Women of all ages, some well past their prime, lug tote bags and umbrellas.

A man is singing opera in front of Charlie's Newspaper Nest. He can be seen at least five nights a week somewhere in the vicinity of the bus depot. Hugo Zacharias, at 70 years of age, belts his favorite stage songs inside the confines and reverberating bulwark of the Hudson Bus Depot. The echoing scales resonate off the glass and concrete walls, intensifying the vocal tension and causing some unrest to the weary commuters while others bravo with amazed cognizance of approval. He begins each practice with a series of better-known opera tics like Carmen or Aida, slowly working in numbers from around the world as throaty, velar phrasings secure more confidence from his captive audience.

Officer Nate Blakely is the patrolman for the Hudson Bus Line District; over the years, he has become the good-cop and bad-cop as well as a running gag straight man to Hugo Zacharias' one-man vaudeville act. Officer Blakely decided to occupy himself with the other side of the depot today. He chose to ignore the dramatic tenor vibrato assonating through the streets and alleyways. Until, of course, he receives a public nuisance report that will leave him no alternative but to respond – sometimes.

Officer Blakely approaches Zacharias in the usual manner, "C'mon, pal. You gotta move it. This is a place of business."

The portly tenor responds in sequence, "I am a place of business. My voice is my business. I have to practice, you know. Be off with you. I am not panhandling, not loitering, I am practicing. Ahh, Venti di mondo facciaa."

Office Blakely retorts, "Yeah, yeah. I know. Take it somewhere else. Sing in the shower like everybody else."

Frustrated, the weary singer raises his fluffy eyebrows in protest, "I live in an apartment. My landlord is a buffoon like, well, let us just say he does not share the same cultural spectrums as say, ahh, someone more dignified and refined as your Uncle, for example, assuming, of course, you do have an uncle. You do, don't you?"

"Cut the bull! C'mon, enough. Let's go."

Jaded to street distractions, Nicolette segues to her block.

Mrs. Glenn is coming up the street with her dog Bingo. Blakely gently hands the man his bag and paperwork as a defeated Hugo Zacharias marches off to his next destination.

A sweeping panorama of storefronts and people on cell phones paint the Avenue. There are no children anywhere, only young adults on scooters and skateboards dressed in skinny jeans and bright sports jackets. Backpacks and laptop computer bags pile up on benches as grizzly-faced males and chubby off-duty receptionists click the keys that open a social world of airwaves and magnetic images. The traffic light changes from yellow to green.

Nicci comes up from the station; she stops at the newsstand and picks up the evening paper. She drops some coins onto the counter and continues walking, enjoying a candy bar. Far away in thought, Nicolette did not notice the little dust mop looking Pekinese brushing the sidewalk beside her.

Mrs. Glenn recognizes Nicci from the apartment. She was always curious about her with the scheduled ins and outs and carrying that gym bag everywhere she went. She was curious also, as neighbors tend to be, about the mysterious young man she spent her time with, the quiet another half that was seldom ever seen.

Mrs. Glenn, being a settled older woman of retirement age, was always curious about what these young people are like. After the death of her husband a few years back, Marsha Glenn resorted to a quiet life tending to Bingo, her dog, and her friends at the church. Things were much different to her now; introducing herself to young people was a welcomed challenge.

After brief eye contact, Nicci addressed the awkwardness, "Well, Hello Mrs. Glenn. I always see you two on your walk, but I never got a chance to say hello." Nicci squatted down and petted

Bingo. "Look at what an adorable ragamuffin you are. Going for a walk around the park?"

"Yes," said Mrs. Glenn. "You can call me Marsha. I am so glad we met. We go for our walk the same time every evening, but I think Bingo just wants to get into the hallway to smell your husband's cooking."

Nicci stood up smiling, still placating the jumping dog. "Oh, that would be Vince. Yes, well, we are not married. Ahh, not yet."

Sensing Nicci's source of discomfort, Mrs. Glenn realizes social norms have changed and it would be more correct not to assume people's situations so quickly.

"I do apologize for being so presumptive. I'm showing my age. But at any rate, how you keep such a gorgeous figure with a man that can cook like that is beyond me. Honey, I gain five pounds just smelling it. And Bingo is already drooling for a biscuit. Well, let us be on our way. I am so glad we finally met. You have a good evening dear."

"Same here, Mrs. Glenn."

Call me Marsha, please. Mrs. Glenn sounds so old."

They both laugh that little laugh that women share just before they go their separate ways.

The sounds of the city subdue as she approaches the brick vestibule to the apartment, fumbling through her bag to find the key. Nicolette opens the door.

The apartment is warm inside; a gentle breeze is blowing from an open window carrying a bracing shot of coolness disturbing the thick controlled climate of radiator heat.

It's a second-floor walkup; there are three bedrooms with a sizable kitchen and enough room for a small table, enabling the remaining space to double as a dining area. The apartment is large for two people; the extra space, however, allows Vincent the needed room for a small art studio and a storage area.

A sense of life and a sense of volume occupy the empty sitting room. There is Bohemian poetry that resonates from the papers and drawings scattering across tables and make-shift easels. Nicco's dance shoes pile in corners next to stacks of books and knick-knack items. A visitor might get an exaggerated idea of things as if looking at a picture in a museum or a voyeuristic glimpse into the artists' life, a feeling so casual that it makes you wonder if any artist believes what he does is art at all, or if he is just acting out a feeling or mood that needs to be expressed all through his walk of life.

Their rooms contain all the controlled clutter and chaos of a youthful busy couple caught in a time of life that holds the right combination of fate and vernalagnia.

Music is flowing from a small radio in the kitchen area where Vince is preparing a meal. The crackling sounds of oil, butter, and eggs, along with a delicate garlic aroma are exuding from the pan. The click, click, click of a knife dices potatoes at sixteen beats per measure. Nicci tosses her bag down with a sigh.

"Hello. Something sure smells good."

Vince turns as they exchange a kiss. Going back to his cooking, he reaches over to grab an egg, missing it slightly. It rolls off the table and breaks on the floor. Vince moves forward to clean the mess, only to notice two egg yolks bleeding from the shell. He returns to the stove.

"Nicci, look a twofer."

Nicci returns to the room, pulling a tee-shirt over her head. "Ummm. What are ya makin'? Looks like potatoes and eggs."

"Yep, frittata—sure is. I hope you're hungry," Vince shakes the pan over the stove.

Nicci looks down at the broken egg, "I'll get this." She carefully begins to slide the double yolk into the paper towel when the sight of the double yolk caused her to panic. "What is the term you say? Morta fame in Italian?"

"Yes."

"Well, I just say feed me around here."

She slides over and gives Vince a peck on the cheek before making her way to the trash to dispose of the broken egg.

"I picked up the bread and the wine you wanted." Nicci was holding the wine preparing to uncork.

Vince looking over his shoulder said, "You know my mother with her old world superstitions right? Say you drop a fork, someone's coming to dinner. You drop a knife, it's bad luck. An egg, especially a twofer, two yolks in one egg meant…"

Before Vince could finish, a crashing bang came from the table.

"Damn!" she said. "Do you believe this? I missed the table. Luckily the bottle didn't break." She regains her coordination and removes the loaf of bread from the bag. "Look, Vince."

Nicci waves a warm loaf of semolina bread in front of Vince, allowing the warm sensuous aroma to permeate his air space.

Vince looks at the bread, shooting a naughty look at Nicci. "Nicolette," he whispered, admonishingly.

Nicci, anticipating his thoughts, sheepishly cut him to the quick. "Yeah, I know, carbs; But I have a craving for little bread and butter if you don't mind."

Vince stops what he is doing and embraces Nicco around the waist. "From what you have been telling me about those scamps around the dance studio, you had better watch every bite."

Vince turns around in a loving caress and moves his hands around her lower back firmly cupping Nicci's ample buttocks.

"Now I don't mind a little cushion for the pushin', but you are the stage dancer in a fancy musical and I shouldn't be selfish about likening this little love handle right here..." He brings his hand around her hip, stroking a slight bump of the underbelly with his thumb.

Nicci playfully pushes him away.

"Wait! Are you saying that I am getting chubby too?"

"Oh, has someone else been taking liberties with your love handles today?" Vince kiddingly starts to tickle her. Remembering the eggs, he steps backward and removes the pan from the flame, pulls her close, and says, "Now where were we?"

Nicco playfully responds to his flirting, as Vince seriously begins taking the light petting to another level.

"No silly; Ozzie mentioned something about working out more. Like, you know, I need to, or something."

Nicci pulled up her tee-shirt, exposing her breasts, as Vince found his way along her hips and mid-section, turning her around allowing her head to roll back along his collar bone. Nicci, feeling a little self-conscious about her sudden weight gain, gets nervous and coy, finding an excuse to pull away.

"I have to wash up before dinner, don't forget about your cooking, and wash your hands, naughty boy."

Vince walks over to the counter and opens the wine. He pours two glasses and suddenly remembers something.

"Nic, I saw Lenny Paxton today. Remember him? We are meeting for coffee tomorrow. He is working with that religious order thing. He sounds happy, a little different, but ok I guess."

Nicci comes in animated, straightening her clothes.

"Oh no, You're kiddin'. Lenny Paxton, wow! Remember when he was playin' gigs at the Roxy? I would never have met you if it was not for him. God, he was so cool and good-looking; then I met you. Gee, what was I thinking? I cannot believe he quit the band scene. He did some studio work for a while I heard. He was the type to play forever. We gonna have him over?"

Vince put out the dishes, bringing the pan to the table. He plates the food while talking.

"I feel a little awkward knowing how he felt about you in those days. If it wasn't a musician groupie crush, then it was love. Lenny was always a kind of a spiritual cat, karma, and all that. When he realized that you and I were in love at first sight, you know what he said? 'I have a fantasy, you have a date with destiny. Go for it.'"

Nicco sat down at the table. She looked at Vince endearingly.

"You never told me that."

"What? That Lenny stepped out of the picture? Sure I did."

"No—the love at first sight thing."

"I couldn't. I was still insecure about losing you to him."

"You felt that way? I am so glad you guys remained best friends. I love you, Vince. I am not a little girl anymore." They kiss and hug.

"But shouldn't I be a little pissed that he gave me up so quickly?" she kidded.

"To the victor go the spoils," Vince held his glass up to toast.

They tap glasses and have dinner.

It was a beautiful afternoon. The sun shone over the buildings, shaping jagged shadows across the boulevard. Tramp pulled himself over the low wall of the Jade Garden restaurant. He made his way cross-town via rooftops to the Buzz Beat Dance Studio. Climbing along with some piping, he nestled under Mrs. Maginty's clothesline just opposite the rehearsal hall window where Ozzie was sitting cross-legged on the floor with some friends from the troupe. Music was playing, and the girls were talking about weekend events, sharing a moment of transcendental escape in between the repetitious workout of their grueling routine.

Carla Davis is third in line under Ozzie Benevento; Ozzie is understudy to Nicolette.

Carla is a tall mocha-skinned Latina. Her broad sculpted face and full lips expose deep roots of African ancestry. She resides temporarily with her mother in a spacious apartment at the lower quarter of east Marin Street, a historic section of town undergoing a cultural renascence. Her mother is a beautician, styling hair for the Upper West Side elite at none other than the chicest of salons, Kasbah. Shaunte Guajardo Davis had to her credit styled and procured, the most infamous coifs from the black and Latino showbiz community, developing a solid reputation amongst her peers. Carla from an early age was privileged to be surrounded by the top names in the local entertainment industry; some have gone on to produce major achievements.

Carla's good looks and stylish appearance got her escorted to many diva performances throughout the club circuit. Her mother, Shaunte, knew where the money was and carefully steered young Carla in its direction.

With gifts of jewelry and meretricious attention from pseudo-celebrity men, it was not long before Carla was diverted from her theatrical career, a vocation she was naturally suited for, and led down the path of vanity and conceit.

Carla at times could be a she-wolf in a lamb's clothing. Playing coy, she got her way through subtle one-up maneuvers, or if need be, just flat-out back-biting. She could at times be smooth and somewhat classy, but there was a neighborhood streak of meanness in her that came through, a hard-wired gene that held her back from her full potential. In her heart, she never fully believed that glory could be had by hard work, blood, sweat, and tears. Her experience showed her that fame, respect, and money came to those who took it by whatever means possible, mostly at the expense of others. Bad habits began to manifest in her from the male companions she frequently acquainted herself with.

A slight flirtation with a recreational narcotic or a promiscuous romp from a friend to a friend became normal for her. It was just a way of doing business. "This was a hip crowd. The rules are different," she would muse.

Things are not always so glitzy for a calendar girl. Being beautiful has certain warning labels attached to it. For instance, beauty could be self-consuming for the person that inherits it. It could outgrow the very host that gives it life taking on a life of its own. It could in some cases pull the self-absorbed into a pool of narcissism and drown them.

In her quiet moments, for example, when Carla was alone with her daydreams in concupiscence, she thought how wonderful it would be to step outside of her body and see herself physically as men saw her. Was she all that they said she was? Was she beautiful; and if so, how beautiful?

She began to develop intolerance to other people, slight envy of anyone that came into her circle. She could be very possessive and vain in her personal life. A gully was opening up in her soul, and it was getting harder and harder to fill it. She was now lurking by the stairwell out of the fraternal loop, focusing her envy on Nicolette Castro.

One of the girls talking with Ozzie noticed Carla approaching and made a note of it to the others.

"Here comes Carla. She has been running her mouth all morning."

Carla became visible to the crowd, swinging her animal print gym bag like a stripper showing up for work. She flashed her large almond eyes around the crowd just once shifting them away behind little slits of long heavy eyelashes.

"Hello, ladies."

"Hi, Carla," Kasey Ogden was the first to shove off. "See you all tomorrow; I got seven minutes to make my train. Oz, don't forget to watch Desert Island tonight. It's the final episode. Tell me who wins. I'm gonna miss it."

"Will do, Kas." The girls exchange a final exit thumbs up and goodbye.

Carla makes her way around Ozzie, who is checking her cell phone messages, an innocuous way to ignore someone without being rude.

Ozzie, feeling her burdening presence, was compelled to acknowledge her.

"Hi, Carla."

Carla cuts to the quick, she is on a mission.

"Word's out you got the understudy part for Ava. Well, lucky you."

Ozzie, sensing the snarky tone to her opening line, shut her cell phone, and started gathering her stuff for an early exit.

"Well, it's not luck. I have been training hard for this, Carla. I was praying for it. Thanks for sayin' anyways."

Carla extends her message in the same jabbing tone. "Relax, girl, you don't have to sweat so hard. It's gonna fall right onto your lap. Your patience paid off."

The other girls, sensing the oncoming drama halfheartedly, fiddled with their cell phones while taking in the subtle digs, rolling their eyes, and fussing with their keypads.

Ozzie, getting annoyed with her cavalier tone, shot back, "Yeah, right. Parts for understudy don't fall, girl, you have to earn them. You should know that by now, shouldn't you, Carla?

"Seen your girl Nicolette before."

"She left a little while ago," Ozzie retorts, a little more relaxed.

"Now that she is eating for two, ain't no wonder you be next in line for that part."

Ozzie huffed and pushed her hair behind one ear. Ozzie was very familiar with this style of innuendo; she looked up for the first time in the conversation.

"Girl, if you got something to say, then maybe you should just say it and be on your way. I don't know what you're talking about."

Carla, stepping back with a flabbergasted look, places her hand across her chest pretentiously playing with her jewelry in mock surprise. "Oh, you ain't heard! Well, excuse me then. Sorry for spoiling the surprise."

Ozzie's patience is wearing thin. This phony playacting is getting to be more than she can stand. The girls are now waiting for the other shoe to drop.

"Carla, go run your mouth to the debutants down the hall. They don't know you as well as we do. This is the pro section all right."

Carla, ignoring her, fluttered her thick eyelashes, and continued with a grin, as if talking to herself.

"Just so happens, that an acquaintance of mine overheard it mentioned, something about a doctor visit this afternoon at the OBGYN. And we know what goes on there. Let's just say that little bulge in the tummy might not be the fault of too many late-night snacks like she is telling everybody."

The girls in the tiny circle look up in shock, unable to speak. Their wide-eyed expressions are a precursor to what is about to unfold.

"Why you think you're gonna get that part, honey? Cause you're all that?" Carla turns to walk away.

Ozzie jumps around and gets in front of Carla, stopping her in her tracks.

"Bitch! You better shut your jealous mouth!" The girls grab Ozzie and pull her over to the corner of the room.

Ozzie, huffing and puffing, could feel the rage well up in her. Being told she had gotten the part under default measures was one thing, but the outward slandering of her best friend for no good reason was insulting to her beyond words. Carla's intent to throw gasoline on a small fire, luring Ozzie into a confrontation, could get Ozzie expelled from the show.

One of the troupe girls held her steady and told her firmly,

"Easy, Oz. It's not worth it. Don't play into it. You have everything to lose, and she has nothing."

Ozzie, still breathing hard, held back with all she had.

"As I said, you a lucky girl."

The hardest thing for Ozzie to accept was Carla's shifty smirk as she walked away with her famous kiss-my-ass-attitude.

Ozzie walks to the window and looks out solemnly thinking, calming down. Below, the streets are sparse with pedestrians. She could see Carla exit the building, daring traffic as she darts across the boulevard. The other performers have heard the commotion and are gathering around. "My God," Ozzie thought to herself, holding back the tears, "My God."

Pond Shark Park, A colloquial nickname for Benson County recreational area has a little man-made lake that glistened beautifully when the sun came up. A picturesque grassy knoll surrounding it is home to a rich fertile soil bed that keeps earthworms and terrestrial gastropods alike, stretched across pedestrian walkways as they slug their way back to an earthen crypt. Starlings with pointed beaks follow them home, pecking for that late morning treat.

Buzzard Park, so named for its ravenous pigeons and ducks, was opposite from the lake, a scenic stretch of county trees and government landscaping.

Bold green and gold signs spaced every thirty feet or so hung from fences, reminding everyone that the taxpayer's dime was being well spent on their comfort. Geometrically placed benches provided ease for seniors and weary nature-buffs resting amongst the laurels.

A local shelter and advocacy organization in the community with an idea for modifying bus stops and park benches decided that instead of trying to discourage a growing homeless population from sleeping on the benches, they'd welcome them to stay. As a result, the collective minds at the municipal think-tank ran a campaign around park benches that folded out like airplane tray tables into miniature shelters.

By day, one version of the bench read, "This is a bench." But at night, the dark revealed a different message, "This is a bedroom."

Carved on almost every wooden frame was initial or hieroglyphic of some kind. Deeply etched marks filled in with rich enamel paint of forest green, ghostly epitaphs from the patrons who have slept there. Some have even advocated for squatters' rights. It was not long before the township elders had to rethink the design for their homeless-friendly bench motels.

The boys at the planning department quickly abandoned the social experiment of collapsible housing in favor of a majority vote for steel dividers that were placed across the seating area, making it impossible for anyone to sleep there.

Lenny was perched on the back of a bench, nostalgically running his finger along a weathered plank, and flicking away some tree bark that shed loose overnight. His angular thin frame added to his skeletal form creating a ghostly specter appearance.

He noticed Vince coming up over the knoll and waved him on. He thought it was good to see Vince again, a familiar face. There are the mixed feelings of breaking away from the tedium of his missionary services, starting new and coming home to the very place he fled from so many years ago, only to soon be off again.

Vince wondered what to expect during his trek over, what to say to his old friend, and how the years and life experiences might have altered them. Both men being of an age when time flies by in a whirlwind, each having had their life experiences intensify, causing segments of memory to get together at times. Larger than life experiences loom like daily occurrences in Len's world, having been all over the globe in the heart of destitute nations. Both parties lived surreal lifestyles. Vince, being an aspiring city artist, and Lenny, a missionary Monk of sorts; it would be difficult in a few compact hours to discern what to take out of the conversation, and what to leave in. Would there still be anything in common to talk about?

However, even though with inner cosmic complexities, Vince did experience that unexplainable thing that happens when true friends reunite. He transformed into a juvenile, meeting his friend in the familiar schoolyard before going off to class. Suddenly, the few extra pounds and a slight maturity of a receding hairline did not matter at all. They hailed, hugged, fist-bumped, and shook.

"Hey, Vince, what is new with the famous artist and sculptor? Now, don't be getting all big on me and stuff. Do you know why I wanted us to meet here? We used to come here as kids. That night when the fog rolled in, and we drank beer under the bridge. You went skinny dipping half crocked, and I had to pull you out because you could not see in the fog."

Vince, sheepishly recalling the incident, cast a look over to the lake. "You were always saving me from something, mostly myself. It's good to see ya again, Len. Hey, it's been too long for old friends to be apart. Nicci and I would love to have you over for dinner. Let's lock it in before we go any further."

Lenny tells Vince in a spirited tone, "It will have to be when I get back ole' buddy. I am leaving for about 6 months. I volunteered to go to Sierra Narvon to help there with the order. That is what I wanted to tell you. I leave tomorrow."

Vince looks quizzical. "Sierra Narvon. Do you like this entire globe-trotting thing, man? When are you going to settle down?"

"You know I love it. I am committed to this, Vince. It helps me write music. I am working on a musical, kind of a rock opera. Besides, I am going to need some artwork. We could talk about it sometime, but right now, tell me how you are getting on with Nicolette. Man, it has been almost 2 years now. Do I hear wedding bells?"

Vince shies away, a little uncomfortable. He knows there should be more progress in this relationship between Nicolette and himself; being torn between careers in the arts and marriage is something that he and Nicci are not able to confront. It is torturing him not to give in.

There are passions embedded for some people, that to be had for all their merit, they must first manifest themselves at precise stages in life. If these signs are missed or not acted upon, they might only leave a ghost of memory for the future, the voided remembrance of a chance not taken.


Vince had tried to apply logic and reason to his relationship with Nicci. Not unlike Rimbaud, he was on an uncharted emotional landscape. The vernorexia that summons up the spirit of mind in a young artist might be explained as a romantic madness, an emotional virus existing for its satisfaction, possessing soulful intelligence like magic or charisma, a demon of disguises—a playful spirit, and a self-destructive imp all in one body.

The Greeks named that deity Eros. The Romans named it Cupid. And though it is proclaimed that love is a universal language, artists, in haste to stroke their ego, do not always recognize another human being as one that needs love also in reciprocity.

At times, it can be an overwhelming passion of the mind that can cause creative people to abandon themselves, giving their souls over to blind love completely.

It is a playful child in a palace where adults can become very serious and draconian. It is a saint in a pagan land where there is no holiness to be found. Hot punks and cool romantics feign poetry in the noonday sun.

Vince, not allowing himself to get trapped, answers directly, "Nicolette loves her dancing and is doing well. She is being considered for a big part in Ava the Dance Production. You may have heard of it. She will probably get it. This is a big step. It could open a lot of doors. Besides, I am selling my work at Prince Gallery across town. I hardly play the guitar anymore. We are happy, Len. We're not talking about marriage yet. I'll tell you all about it over a cup of coffee."

—Across town...

The sign outside the door was hand-painted, "Granary Grill." Inside, the tables were spaced, and comfortable seating arrangements offered the two girls privacy to discuss the pending problem. Nicolette is twisting her napkin, staring into the ice formation of her diet soda. The waitress stops by to drop off a plate of sliced lemon. Ozzie runs her fork through a few French fries floating in a pool of ketchup. The ice in Nicci's glass pops, acting as a starting gun to begin her talking.

"Ozz, I don't know what to say. I don't know what to do."

"You have to tell Vince, Nic. You have to tell Vince,"

Nicolette shifts, lifting her head.

"He's going to want me to have the operation. I can't do that, Ozz. The counselor said we could discuss options; I could bring in the 'baby's daddy' or some such snarky cliché, and of course, the old standby. No one would have to know. I cannot pretend like that, not with something like this. Vince would freak if he ever found out. My mother would never understand. Oh, my God. I am destroying everyone I love." Nicolette holds the twisted napkin to her face and begins to cry.

Ozzie stretches a comforting hand across the table, offering the inner understanding and compassion women have been sharing and suffering for thousands of years, the bond of inner spirit that neither circumstance nor men have ever been able to dismantle: the cult sisterhood that allows women to transcend all religion and propriety.

Divine is the Goddess in a threadbare coat; however, Ozzie fears in her own heart the experience and earthly wisdom she lacks at this moment is about to overwhelm her.

The effect is likened to a dream sequence, a surreal garden that has no setting of flowers, no background of walls or path, just the stark reality of being, devoid of meaning and miracles.

Ozzie is consciously aware of her limitations.

"Nic, it's ok. It looks big now, but it is going to be alright. Baby steps, Nic, take baby steps. Oh my God. I didn't mean it that way."

Nicci lets out a banshee moan, "Ohh!" she holds her head with both hands. "Vince would marry me tomorrow. He loves me. I believe that. He is not completely into the organized religion thing. I am not ready for that either. My dancing means everything to me, but I want to have this baby."

Ozzie looking on bites her lip, her eyes gently tear up overflowing. She knows what having a baby now would mean to her career, to the show. The two friends lean forward and hug over the table almost knocking over the French fries.

"I wish there was something I could say, Nic. This sucks."

Nicolette pulls back, straightens, gathers energy, and now comforts Ozzie.

"There is. Take my part in Ava. I will drop out. I'll come up with something. Don't let Carla weasel you out of it, Ozz; you deserve it. She is already undermining, one of her lackey friends was hanging around the doctor's office. After all, this settles down, I could get back into the show. We could still work together." Nicolette halfheartedly believed anything she just said.

"Nic, I feel so terrible. I know we have not known each other very long, but I learned so much from you. I am happy for you and Vince. I am so sad because I know how much…" Ozzie begins weeping uncontrollably. In a sudden role reversal, Nicolette is comforting Ozzie, who has just fallen apart. Nicco, holding Ozzie's shoulder, wipes her eyes and some ketchup that has gotten on Ozzie's forearm.

"I know, honey. I know. Please, stop," Nicolette hands her a tissue. "One of us has to be the strong one."

Ozzie blows her nose, then Nicolette blows her nose. People are beginning to look around. Nicolette, becoming more aware of the attention they are attracting, self-consciously looks around; she picks up the check and escorts Ozzie, who can barely compose herself, to the door.

Two rabbis seated a few tables away look up at the commotion. Rabbi Crivitz is sitting having coffee with a fellow teacher, Albert Kohn, when Crivitz asks, "Did they say they are getting married? Is that legal?"

Albert Kohn replies, "Who knows? These kids today, first they say marriage is overrated, now look what you have."

# PRINCE GALLERY-VINCENT GALLE

An anorexic tall, thin woman dressed completely in black is paused looking at a series of paintings that are regimented along a small strip of wall space at the corner of a large white room. She has the arm and ear of a well-dressed man in a classic dark blue Brooks

Brothers suit. They are accompanied by a portly gentleman in a pale blue velour jogging outfit. The girl is an international art buyer and office space consultant representing the firm Goodman and Ritchie, a design team that purchases art from gallery artists with the intent of decorating offices, banks, and large institutions with artwork from up and coming to no-name artists. They hope to promote the artist into commercial success, thereby increasing the value of their clients' investment. "Junk bonds, you can hang on your wall," as Vince was heard mumbling into the ear of an Asian buyer one dismal evening at Gallery Zink.

Vincent had a proclivity towards off-the-cuff statements at inopportune times, sometimes jeopardizing art sales. Off-setting the mood of self-important patrons who were over enjoying their role as chic financiers of the art world supplied him a baleful pleasure. His "Give to Caesar what is Caesar's and give to the artists what is the artists" manner became a nuisance to many gallery owners around the area; so much so that some have refused to handle his work, while others just shunned the mere mention of his name.

In this environment, one did well to play along and not allow artistic temperament to spoil the party. Money and fame were being made. Quick cash was lucrative on the inside. Even the staunchest bohemians were known to be traveling with thirty grand rolled up in their sock. Fame and celebrity status was being created so quickly that paintings were sold before the paint could dry properly.

Renaissance masters have not ever experienced the pop idol stardom and pampering that celebrity cult worshippers were bestowing over their new lovelies. The young woman in black was holding a wine glass cupped in both hands as the chubby gentleman in the jogging suit slowly pushed a flaky hors d'oeuvre into his anxious mouth.

Vincent's artwork was on display. Presented were lofty images in fields of color transparencies, soft illuminations shimmer through the illusion of pigment and texture, with a careful balance of value and line. The soulful compositions bring mild hypnosis to the viewer, peacefulness, sometimes breaking into a rapturous overflow of twists and circle strokes injecting push-pull and counterbalance. One had the experience of an unexpected visitor disturbing a peaceful dream.

The Color of Sleep is the name of the show; the guests are now arriving to witness it.

The Prince Gallery is the child of Damien Polhause and his partner Andrew Knight. Prince Gallery is a struggling attempt by Polhause and Knight to break into that world of lucrative money and easy living.

In the mindset spirit of most Romantic inclined people, there is sometimes an attempt to recapture nostalgia from a previous era. Andrew Knight came up from a generation that was gutted and loose, a cultural zealot from a city that broke rules. He always teetered on the edge like a rising politician or athlete, never envisioning himself as the champ but always as a worthy contender. He would fight the good fight always rewarding himself at the end of the day with a party to attend.

Damien Polhause, on the other hand, was a mid-western boy on his own, escaping the small minds of a no-name town where he was the only homosexual, so he was told, mostly by closet homosexuals. He was brought up in a culture-conscious protestant family well connected with town politics. Throughout his youth, Damien always pursued the theater and began writing plays for small venues. However, he maintained a stubborn streak for taboo subjects that brought him even more isolation and dismay.

Recognizing there was a demand for art and design in the theater districts, he started a small agency that pulled together artists and designers. He eventually answered a call to go east and try his hand at gallery management, where he met Andrew Knight, who was pontificating on the wooden floor at a city hall meeting advocating for better rent control. Damien was processing their forms and building code information for property leases concerning his new Prince Gallery. The two opposites attracted and now they share a gallery.

Vincent's abstracts are vibrating the walls. The soft soothing color fields are getting the attention of prospective buyers. Chaperones are servicing the room clad in black pants and crisp white shirts offering guests prosecco and Lillet. Against the back wall was a low table with a large pyramid of every kind of Belgian chocolate imaginable.

Damien Polhause is talking with a group of collectors, convincing them that falling in love with a Galle painting is the first requisite to purchasing it. A photographer is taking pictures of an effete Damien alongside a husky middle-aged woman in a tawny dress, adorned with heavy baubles dangling from her neck and wrist. Damien checks his watch, casting a sly sideward glance to the concierge door fellows manning the front and back exits. He receives a negative nod. No Vincent as of yet.

Five minutes past showtime, he adjusts his clothing, internalizing an uneasy contre parry, shifting away from the inevitable questions he will soon be asked by everyone who approaches him, "Has Vincent arrived yet? Can I meet the artist? Will you introduce us?" Damien feigns a smile that exudes pure effervescence, sighing off camera a puff of uncertainty. Now what? Where is he?

The back alley behind the Prince Gallery is not as idealistic as the front and interior. Stray cats and rather large vermin scatter away as Vincent rolls his thin Honda motorcycle between a dumpster and a sleek Mercedes. The car is the sole property of Andrew Knight, on loan to Damien for the weekend. Andrew is away attending an art opening for a controversial new artist named Casper Wyatt.

Wyatt's art is a series of photographs and paintings featuring women ranging from teenage years to the elderly, some decrepit sprouting dowager humps tied and bound with rope and cords of all thickness and texture displaying many intricate knot forms. The varying knot forms offer texture, shaping, and design to the rope, which is what the artist wants the viewer to focus on. The bondage of the models, however bound and sadistically tied, is open to one's interpretation. Some male models are also displayed in various shackles and face masks. That being said, holding to form, the knotting is superb.

Vincent shuts down his bike and looks over the Mercedes. He slowly lowers his eyes to the license plate as he walks past. The plate reads KNIGHT 2 REMBR. Vincent reached up over his head and grabbed onto the fire escape ladder. He pulled it down and began to ascend toward the roof, slightly slipping on his pointy Italian shoes. Once up top, he lightly walked over to the skylight window overlooking the gallery floor. He sat crouched over a nest of bricks to examine the crowd below.

He observed Damien checking his watch, dialing his cell phone. Within a few seconds, Vincent's cell phone rang. Vincent reached into his jacket pocket without ever taking his eyes off Damien. He held the phone in his hand and truncated the call with the press of his thumb. Vincent smiled, watching Damien stare into his phone, frustrated with irritation. Vincent observed the crowd a little longer, enjoying his stint of voyeurism.

One well-dressed man who carried himself as more important than any painting in the room grabbed at the hors d'oeuvres tray, startling the server who had to struggle to keep it balanced on her hand.

Small cabals of beautiful women accompany well-to-do older men and circle the room waltz-like. Couples of all sorts are hanging on each other's arms. Glamorous, ritzy personalities, along with tweed and bow tie academics alike make small talk.

Vincent observes a few seconds longer, smiles to himself, stands, and walks toward the edge of the roof. He looks over the horizon of tenements and buildings. Audiences of vagrants are watching him from a neighboring ally. In an unsuitable gesture, Vincent pounds his chest like Tarzan and begins to howl in yodeling tones, primitive sounds repeated in rapid changes of pitch.

He quickly about faces, climbs back down the fire escape, and jumps onto the street, pausing for a moment to check his hair in the motorcycle rearview mirror. He then proceeds calmly around the building to the gallery entrance. The concierge recognizes him signaling to Damien.

Damien immediately bum rushes Vincent at the entrance and leads him off to an office. He anxiously rushes Vincent through the door locking it behind him.

"Vince, fashionably late is one thing, but seriously, where have you been? Do you see them out here? These potential buyers are waiting to meet you. These are your patrons. Look at you! You're a mess! Let me see your nails. You are not drunk or anything, are you? Where did you get those hideous shoes?"

Vince could not help succumbing to the gentle adulation; he drew a cold comfort from it, recalling an indiscretion of youth when he was being reprimanded by his mother over a graduation party incident many years ago. Vincent answered in a schoolboy rebel tone, "No."

"Are you nervous? Do you remember what I told you?"

Vincent answers in the same deadpan manner, "Yes."

"Yes, what? Nervous or you remember?"

"No, not nervous. Yes, I remember."

Coach Damien replies, "Nod and smile! Nod and smile! Remember the less said, the better; now go get 'em."

Damien adjusts his clothing, allows a second to compose, and escorts Vincent out to the gallery floor.

Damien steps out of the door and is immediately greeted by the portly woman in the yellow-brown dress.

Vincent wedged between the door and Damien struggles to straighten. He is being crushed between Damien and the fat woman.

Damien, acting as nonchalant as ever, exclaims in surprise, "Oh Mrs. Hamish! I'm so glad I found you again. I promised to tell you the first thing when the artist arrived. I did not forget you. Vincent, this is Megan Hamish. You know she founded banally last spring. What a success that was, Meg. I am sure we can make it happen again. Not quite the same way, but probably better."

Nicolette is one of the two people who Tramp trusts enough to enter the dwelling. The other is Mrs. Tandem on Hobart Avenue, who leaves the window open when Tramp arrives, then leaves the room. Tramp lets himself out after a few nibbles to show Mrs. Tandem that her efforts were not in vain. Tramp was considerate that way.

Nicolette was pacing back and forth. The slight murmur of a meow from the closed window awakened her from her troubled thoughts. She opened the window and Tramp leaped onto the counter sniffing the air for familiar smells.

"Hey Tramp, old friend; where you been?"

Nicolette walks over to the cupboard, gets a can of cat food out, opens it, and puts it in a dish she keeps on the fire escape. Then pouring some milk into a dish, places it in front of Tramp.

The cat slurps at the food and drink. When Tramp is finished, Nicolette picks him up and gently rocks him like a baby, singing sweetly in his ear. Nicolette sings, "Hush, baby, don't you cry, Momma's gonna sing you a lullaby. And if that lullaby doesn't sing, mamma's gonna buy you a diamond ring. And if that…" Before she could finish, she starts to cry.

In doing so, she squeezes the cat uncomfortably, causing him to jump out of her arms and go back through the window. Nicolette turns and walks over to the computer. She sits down and stares at the screen where the research was already in progress. Hesitating, she slowly begins to type. She types of PROCEDURE. Nicolette's eyes are moving as she reads; her eyes are as big as saucers.

The chemical blue from the screen outlines her face. The anodyne hue produces an unnatural pallor not produced in nature casting a ghostly visage over her face and torso. She types another entry. She becomes more intense. She hesitates, types, and tension builds. The word IMAGE flashes on the computer screen. Nicolette's eyes look down at the keyboard, she taps the key.

Her eyes open wide aghast. She throws herself back in the chair her hand covering her mouth in horror. At that moment, her concentration splits apart as the phone rings breaking the dead silence. She shrieks and jumps, then falls back regaining her composure. She lets it ring out.

She picks up the phone, and looking at the face dial, a familiar sequence of numbers appears. Breathing a sigh of relief, Nicolette holds the phone to her chest whimpering to herself the name Sonia.

A collective exuberance veils the city at certain hours of the evening. This is the time that most taxi drivers wait for all day.

There is no specific starting bell for this or exact science to explain it—just an intuitive call to action that folks in the service industry understand. For instance, concierges adjust their attire; bartenders dust idle glasses that gather lint from a slow afternoon. Maintenance people check the neon lights on marquees and windows assuring all fixtures are in place and functioning. The striptease Cantonese, for example, displays elaborate lighting of exotic women welded from neon tubing to the shape of a dancing native Hawaiian girl; the body is yellow light, the dress blue. It is an original design first installed after WWII, in part, to entertain the shore-leave memories of some troops that have served in our campaign against the Japanese. Many classical designs in neon still exist. Considered tacky by some, they still perform a very elementary function. They lure in curious working-class stiffs all dressed-up with nowhere to go, searching for the legend of flight and fantasy that is Saturday night

A cop is directing traffic. A man is buying tickets for a play as his attractive female companion looks around bored.

People are sitting in a coffee shop working on laptops, some reading books, some are arguing.

Two cooks are slamming woks in the kitchen of the Jade Chinese restaurant. You could hear them through the backdoor chirping; an argument might be brewing, or they could just be telling jokes.

Men are going into nightclubs and bars. A couple on a romantic rendezvous is arguing in the street. Temperatures are running hot from tenement Romeos to waitresses and barmaids preparing to work the late-night shift; the girl upstairs with the perfumed hair has a lash of strawberry blond in her eye, and it's annoying the hell out of her.

"We got an easy job," someone said, pulling in that last fare.

"I don't give a rat's ass," someone answered back. "I just want to get out of work".

"Everyone is where they are supposed to be, everywhere and nowhere at the same time. We will be driving around in circles all night."

Vince, coming up the steps, opens door to the faintly lit apartment, goes in, and turns on the light. Nicolette is lying on the floor with broken glass next to her. She is unconscious. Vince looks around suspiciously for any intruder. Everything is in order; no sign of foul play.

"Jesus! Nic," he takes her hand making her sit up.

Nicci begins to revive, groans, holding her head, and mumbles, "Oh! Vince, I don't know I got so light-headed."

Vince brings a chair over, helps her up, and sits her down on the chair. He gets a wet cloth and wipes her head and face.

"Oh! Vince," slightly disoriented. "I must have fainted. I just hung up the phone with my sister Sonia. I got up for some water. The last thing I remember is getting dizzy, and that was it. Ouch. I must have banged my head."

Vince, attending to her, hears the phone ring just behind him, but ignores it. Letting the answering machine take it, he focuses his attention on Nicolette. Nicolette is still foggy.

The phone rings again with an annoying inopportune tempo. Nicolette waves her hand as she helps herself to her feet.

"Let the answering machine take it. The damn thing has been ringing all night, mostly for you. And did you go to the opening? Damien has been calling every 5 minutes. Why don't you just answer your cell?"

"I forgot it," he confessed.

A phone message comes over the speaker, half in Spanish and broken English.

"Nicolette, it's me, Mamma. Your sister called. Why you don't tell me these things? I worry, you know. You make me crazy. I have to talk to this machine. I'm your mother. Show a little respect. Sonia told me about the doctor. I'll come down, and we can help. Don't worry. Your sister is good at this. She knows. Talk to her. You never tell us anything. All right, you're probably sleepin'. Call me back." The echo of a click sounded across the room.

Vince, feeling out of the loop, asks, "What is she talking about, Nic? What is going on? Are you alright?"

"Give me a minute, Vince. Just a minute," Nicolette crawls around slowly regaining equilibrium. "I am pregnant, Vince. I went to see the doctor. It is confirmed."

Vince almost knew what she was going to say.

"When were you going to tell me? Damn Nic, what are we going to do? Nicci, we gotta think about this. I mean, we gotta think about this!"

"There's not a lot to think about, Vince. I am having it."

"Nicci, this is a beautiful thing for some folks, but not us. We are both too selfish. We cannot do this. You're dancing, my work. Who is going to handle all this? The feeding, the peeing, the crying. I can't even change a diaper. What are you going to do when..."

"Vince, stop! I know how you feel, but I am having this baby. If you love me, I mean really love me, you would..."

"Go ahead, Nic. What? Marry you? That magic solution will make everything better. Make your mother happy. Legitimize this thing of ours."

"You could be supportive instead of being a selfish jerk. I never saw this side of you."

"We are selfish jerks, Nicci! That is why you dance, that is why I paint. It's hard to succeed at what we do without being selfish."

Nicci cries and Vince grabs his coat.

"I have to take a walk." Vince half walks away, confused. He tries to hug her, but she pushes him away.

"I did not say anything about marriage, Vince. Marriage is a trial of good times and bad times. I could never marry someone who jumps ship so easily. I thought I knew you better."

They look intensely at each other.

"Vince, one more thing. Just stay with me until the baby is born, O.K?"

Vince walks out quietly.

There is a macadam path off Veterans Boulevard; large slates line the street, just before it turns into an old cobblestone parking lot. A small crowd has gathered to watch a street artist sketch out a drawing onto a slab of slate. The drawing appears to be a type of iconic Madonna and Child replica of a popular old masterwork.

The artist rubs a cloth on his chalk-stained hand as he draws, rubs, and blends around an eye. He skillfully moves his hand, placing a well-determined line, shaping it into form then blending it to shade and texture.

As the artist is working over his picture, kneeling on the pavement, his hand is smudging the edge of the infant's mouth; he softens the cheek with a steady finger.

An empty coffee pot collects donations, enough hopefully to keep him in supplies. Maybe there's enough left over for a cold beer and some grub at the end of the day.

He mindfully tips his hat to the clink of coins dropping in as by-passers look on with admiration. Without warning, thunder rumbles. Storm clouds appear producing lightning; it begins to rain.

People scatter around to seek shelter from the cloud burst. The more prepared, they have open umbrellas; some duck into stores.

An old man with a pipe looks up aloof to the sky as the rain hits his face.

A homeless person covers his humble cart with plastic as he scrambles toward a nearby gazebo.

Pedestrians are hailing cabs; one well-dressed woman climbs into the back seat of a taxi protecting her new hat with a newspaper.

The anonymous street artist gathers his things into a duffle bag, grabs his tip can, and hustles off.

The chalk drawing is incomplete. The colors are running off the slate, the image is slowly dissolving from the rain. Watercolor puddles spill out over cracks and crannies forming cloudy wells of color along the boulevard.

## LENNY PAXTON
## SIERRA NARVON

-From the journal of Lenny Paxton. Late spring Sierra Narvon jungle heat

-101 d.

-Tuesday

How could it be that various people, different from one another, remote from each other, separated by land and sea, should form similar social groups based on what would seem to be a human social invention, the ownership of land? The survival value that territory brings to species varies as widely as do the opportunities of species themselves.

I came across this passage from a published journal I found here. It struck a nerve with me about what might be missing. Places and motivations do not seem to change much. I am on the other side of the world. Survival still suffers the same basic rules.

-Wednesday
Concerning my Rock Opera (Untitled as of yet)
I now have a collection of songs with various plot strains, consistent characters, and a score. Still moving toward some sort of rock opera/musical theatre thing.
It's not that I had a burning desire; it's just that my obsessive nature created a basic group of works. I need to get back to the city and work again.

Concerning E…I love her with all my heart. I will ask her to come along, but it will be difficult. She is committed to her work here. I will try to persuade her.
Maybe if I ask her to marry me?

The warm wood and mortar building cools in the morning shade; it casts a shadow over the garden where Lenny Paxton turns over soil and sod. He is preparing a healthy mix of fertilizer and raw dirt. Every morning, he toils for an hour or so planting crops that will nourish Emily and him, not to mention the children who look forward to snacking on the fresh fruits and vegetables provided at the schoolhouse farm recreation area.
The Red House, as they call it, is a school for the children of the town. It is separated from the settlement by a large acreage of the plotted field providing corn and wheat.
Each day, a meal is provided and a basic introduction to reading, math, and basic skills. When the children's studies are complete, they have a recreation period, where they are permitted to play on

swings and form teams to play a competitive sport on their spacious makeshift sports field.

This week, however, the school is quiet and closed for a solstice break. Sierra Narvon is centered on an agricultural community; many of the farmers need to have their children help them on their farms a week or two out of the year. It is the third world and poor, but making great strides due to volunteer groups dispersed to the area.

Lenny is an American working with a charitable Franciscan order. His partner, Emily Harrell, comes from the United Kingdom; she teaches music and English and is affiliated with the League of Mercy Sisters at Program Square One, also a volunteer group. They have worked together for a year and a half before deciding to part ways with the order residency in town and reside at the school, referring to it as their "squatter's paradise."

The upstairs compartments were a kitchen with running water and a bedroom with a smaller room off to the side. That became the administrative office for the school's business. Half the building had electricity, and the other half did not. The school itself had a piano for Emily and some donated string instruments that allowed Lenny to work on his music.

There were many instances when Lenny questioned the composition of his life. There were times when the old wooden floor and the many neglected windows were dirty and hard to look at, symbols of abject poverty. At other times, a ray of light might beam through one window, in particular, declaring sovereignty over all the other things. It was not the bareness of the empty rooms, but the lack of clutter that made it handsome to him. Humanity suffers, but it is the dignity we bring to life. Stateliness we create in ourselves. It was in these rooms that he realized the dust on the old wooden floor had a past, a present, and a future; its story was his story, a story that Emily was a very big part of.

He had learned from Vince that a painting, which looks simple, might have taken a wartime effort from the soul to complete. It is with the natural order of things.

❦

Emily steps out onto the plank board floor porch welcoming the morning. On days like today, when there are no classes to be held, Emily extends the luxury of primping a little extra. Her daily attire is simple for the desert-dwelling: khaki cargo pants, short sleeve Oxford shirt, and buck boots. Her hair is usually up in a bun extending her neck about two solid inches above her shirt collar. She is a true ectomorph, long and lean. Her daily rigorous chores and almost completely vegan diet keep her from ever gaining any extra weight. Her wardrobe consists of two sundresses that she brought with her from England and a few sun hats.

This morning, however, she is wearing for the first time a beautiful Dashiki dress that was made for her by a woman from the village. Adjoa Bolade, a local seamstress, cut, dyed, and procured the fabric herself, before offering it to Emily as a gift for the long hours spent, tutoring her in English.

The clinging gauze wrapped around her waist as the gentle desert breeze lifted the edges about her legs gently outlining her elongated muscular thighs. Thin strips of leather adorned her neck. She was veiled in the colors of an aurora sky. Her flaxen hair was half hung down from an unfastened bun being held loosely together by a colorful comb sculpted from animal bone.

Emily made herself comfortable at a small wood table at the corner of the porch. She was sipping tea and fanning herself with a local news publication. The news in these parts is scant and slow, producing an eagerness in foreigners to consume newsworthy items. Emily had subscriptions from the British News-Herald and the Daily Star; that she would pick up in town, but they took forever to get delivered. She was able to get clear internet off her laptop; however, the virus problem became too difficult to ward off. Eventually, she resigned herself to the reality that she will have to catch up on the news after it happens.

She was quickly caught by the headline.

ROVING THIEVES STILL AT LODGE, SUSPECTED OF AT LEAST 3 KNOWN ATTACKS NEAR AND AROUND CONYAN REGION. BE ADVISED.

-DANGEROUS. POLICE ARE IN THE AREA.

Emily looked at Lenny tending the garden. Shading her eyes with her hand, she searches into her backpack for sunglasses. After finishing her tea, Emily walked over to the spacious outdoor shower enclosure behind the building. This was a gated separate section a short distance behind the school. Lenny constructed it a short time after they decided to commune as one.

A manual pump provided running water as long as the tank is full. Emily hoists a wooden bucket of distilled rainwater into the tank and proceeds to pump the lever, generating enough pressure for a quick shower. The wooden chamber somewhat crude is well built, spacious, and sturdy, providing privacy and a decent level of comfort. A perforated fiberglass roof is translucent enough to provide enough natural sunlight and allow soft desert breezes to soothe.

Emily steps into the shower and removes her clothes, hanging them behind a plastic curtain. Behind the curtain is a shelf that holds soap and toothpaste along with two cups labeled Lenny and Emily.

Emily was not one to afford herself too many luxuries, but she did, however, keep two things sacred: her tea and her soap. There is a special blend soap Emily has been using for as long as she can remember. Her favorite pet luxury is to have it delivered from a specialty shop in Wiltshire England, not far from where she grew up… The floral aromatics bring to mind her mother and sisters at holiday coming in from the marshes holding armfuls of freshly picked heather. A bit of homesickness wells up, as a scant tear runs down her face.

Emily thought to herself. Even if she did decide to spend her life with Lenny and she did live in America, she would still be an ocean away from home, another form of exile.

She turns a crude pressure valve that releases the water and begins her shower, soaping up her hands and face. A delicate scent of lavender English soap escapes through the shower door, transcending on a balmy cloud passing over Lenny, momentarily distracting him.

A mere, meager whiff some distance away is enough to arouse the primal sensuality that corrupts his senses.

Small flirtations with human nature such as these awakened Lenny to the reality that although his spirit was willing, his flesh would never be able to endure the pious life of a holy man. His past indoctrination to the world tainted him severely, having long since destined for him the road he was to follow, and it was an earthly one. The thoughts of returning home were becoming more intense. He wanted Emily to share life with him.

Lenny had with him a small outdated battery-operated cassette player he kept for when life on the plain became unbearable. He was able to salvage a few tapes from local markets in town. Switching it on, a familiar rock song soon drowned out the rustling disturbance of the cornfields around him.

Lenny stands wiping his brow and takes a swig of water from his canteen. He looks out over the tall vegetation beyond his garden.

There is a slight rustling of branches and a young boy comes out of the bushes.

Lenny does not recognize him as a student from the school. Then, two others emerge holding sticks. They surround him in seconds.

The life of a Lowlands Plains officer is hard and mean. It is not much different than a missionary worker in the sense that many of these officers are dedicated lawmen. Some have come up through the ranks with a dedication to doing justice; some are no better than paid mercenaries looking to earn a buck. Most often, they are committed law enforcers with a true concern for local safety. Some ex-military men have come as far away as Australia and New Zealand to escape the routine predictable outcomes of their outback regions choosing to fill their time and sadistic proclivities with more dangerous untamed settings.

The Sierra Narvon law enforcement building is set off of the main road called Claxton. It is more familiar to the parallels of a road map than it is to anyone familiarly describing its location. All roads in these areas are rural and only accessible by jeep or all-terrain vehicles. The locals, however, travel mostly on foot or caravan and are warned not to deviate from the main roads. Gangs of thieves and vagrants gather in the jungles along outposts prying on unaware travelers.

On the wall of the law enforcement building just outside the police chief's office is a sign that reads,

> "The bylaws of Sierra Narvon lays down that the South Continent Police Service has a responsibility to prevent, combat and investigate crime, maintain public order, protect and secure the inhabitants of the Republic and their property, uphold and enforce the law, create a safe and secure environment for all people in Sierra Narvon, prevent anything that may threaten the safety or security of any community, investigate any crimes that threaten the safety or security of any community, ensure criminals are brought to justice, and participate in efforts to address the causes of crime."

Sierra Narvon police officers on duty generally carry a Vektor Z88 9mm pistol, although a more compact pistol, the rap 401 is available if officers request it, and pepper spray, while officers in Sierra Narvon along with some other services of the force are equipped with Glock 17. Each police patrol usually also equipped an r5 rifle in the car.

To quell disturbances, the SAP used a variety of arms, including R1 semi-automatic rifles, BXP sub-machine gun, and a musler 12 gauge shotgun which is capable of firing the new generation of anti-riot rubber bullets, which are contained in a standard 12 bore shotgun cartridge, as well as tear gas grenades using a so-called ballistic cartridge and pencil flares.

Police chief Bheki Kwazake rolls back in his chair looking out of his window to watch patrol vehicle 4 roll-off leaving a cloud of dust. Four vehicles have been dispersed in the vicinity of the public schoolhouse three miles away.

Three patrolmen, armed with rifles, are looking out over the dusty plain. One of them notices an unnatural path in the stalk field, suspicious bends, and breaks along the formation. He motions to the driver, who pulls over. The other officer gets off the vehicle, casting a keen eye over the field. He notices a fresh-cut trail that has been coarsely severed, probably by machete; some footprints were also left in a sandy area along the trail.

He makes notes and relays the info to the driver.

A patrolman in a second vehicle simultaneously flanking the area reports another observation.

"Call for backup. It looks like the trail breaks off here. They cut through the woods. Tell headquarters to send some back up to the schoolhouse on the other side of the brush. There could be six of them, maybe more." Over the radio, a squelching voice breaks the loss of clicks and frequency glitches.

"That building is a missionary outpost. The report has a man and a woman living on it."

The first officer reports, "We have been tracking these bandits for 3 days now; this is the only place they can stop in this radius for food and water. I hope we are not too late."

The two jeeps are about a mile from each other; they coordinate quickly and race off in perpendicular directions. A broken signpost splinters in the wake of tires spinning; the red schoolhouse lies on the horizon.

Even with the cloudy shade of a translucent roof, the jungle sun was intense enough to vaporize drops of water from Emily's shoulders. Wrapping the towel around her, she grabbed her clothes from behind the curtain gently reaching forward, unlocking the door.

As she stepped from the shower, she was startled by a wiry gangly man. Pushing her backward, he covered her mouth with his hand, her pale blue eyes widened with fear as she locked eyes with a killer. His eyes floated like dark cherries isolated and alone in a bowl of buttermilk. The sinister still life experience was the last composition her mind would allow her to create before fear took over forcing her to act.

She reached behind herself grabbing the cup with Lenny's name on it, bringing it down on her assailant's head. Not flinching, he holds her still while another man with a gun across his back stares at her, as a third man pointed a rifle at her.

Two patrol jeeps are getting ready and pulling away from headquarters. The officer on the CB radio is talking with the first dispatched unit already en route to the schoolhouse. A burly officer in outfit fatigues ties a bandanna over his mouth to protect his face from the road dust blowing up from the wheels.

The first jeep is racing through, causing the tires to spin digging into broken branches and off-road debris.

"I hope we are not too late," he whispers.

The wiry man drags Emily from the shower, as the others surround her. She struggles but only briefly. The men begin pushing her back and forth from one to the other, brutally trying to get her attention; one of them grabbed her by the hair to hold her head still. He squeezed her face so roughly the inside of her cheek began to bleed. The man looked into her eyes studying them; the luminosity of her pale blue iris was frightening him. The first man ripped at her towel. Naked and frightened, Emily feared to resist, waiting instead for a moment to escape.

The two bandits force her into the schoolhouse. The third kept watching outside. He hears a jeep coming up from the road and steps out in front of the house to get a better look.

Flanked off the side of the field about 30 yards away, commander Dooley, a trained ex-military man, focuses his scope onto the bandit that was watching out. Dooley, an excellent marksman, was studying the later half of the episode waiting patiently for the gunmen to come into a clearing; he watches through his scope observing the predator. Distracted, the bandit searched in confusion for intruders. With the firm squeeze of the trigger, a bullet whistled through the air, finding its mark in the bandit's chest. The bandit tumbled back from the impact of the shell, a dull thud sounded as he hit the ground—a puff of dust rose from beneath his body. The others in the schoolhouse had no idea he was down.

From the direction of the garden area, Dooley heard a shot fired. He contacts the flank officers at the garden side instructing them to move in with caution. A shrill voice breaks over the radio, "A pedestrian was shot.

-Assistance on the way. Proceed with caution, assailants armed and dangerous."

Lenny looks up from the garden scanning the tall stalks; some boys are cutting their way through with a machete, the tops of their heads are undulating in a wave, their dark pates contrasting against the golden grain. A star-like glimmer reflects off the tip of a metal object as they came closer into the clearing. Lenny noticed the strap of a rifle dangling from a young boy's shoulder. The other boys had sticks and one wielded the machete.

It was too late when Lenny noticed these were not mission boys from the village. After standing up, he was surrounded.

They began beating him with sticks and the blunt end of the machete struck him across the legs. He fell to the ground like a wounded animal. His head was heavy, and he began to fade in and out of consciousness from the repeated blows. He reached out trying to grab a stick, hoping to pull it away from the boy; if he could secure a weapon, he could better defend himself. A shot went off.

Lenny felt the hot sting of lead enter his midsection.

He could tell that it passed completely through him from the excruciating pain he felt in his back as the bullet exited.

His last thought was of Emily. Screaming her name, he twisted and turned one last time before a club-like object struck his skull.

It was a blind miracle; jeeps began to roll in from the bush seemingly out of nowhere. The boy with the gun fired wildly, that was the shot piercing Lenny through the midsection. The officers jumped from their vehicles brutally subduing the bandits, cuffing them and holding them to the ground. The boy with the gun began waving his weapon. He was laughing. The silliness in his expression was that of one who was mildly retarded, perhaps not fully grasping the weight of what was going on. He looked as though he was playing a game that no one was taking seriously. He was shot dead immediately. That laughing child was the last thing Lenny remembered before he passed out.

The police formed a semi-circle surrounding the schoolhouse where Emily is held captive. They flank the doors and windows while two armed riflemen prepare to go inside. Approaching with caution, the officers signal to each other; they stealthily go through the room between the thin plank board walls; dull breathing could be heard escaping from between the cracks.

The door swings open, one of the bandits steps out armed and is immediately shot multiple times.

Glass is shattering as a bandit is getting picked off from sniper fire on the other side of the captives' room; the heavy thump of bodies hitting the floor, one, then two, then silence.

"We know that there is someone else in there," Dooley reasoned to himself.

In Dooley's mind, a mind that was not inexperienced or jaded in any way to the brutality and bloodshed that one might expect to find behind closed doors, thoughts drifted to Holiday with his wife Pamela and his daughter Chloe visiting the Cape of Hermanus, picnicking on the shore; Chloe, running toward him from the beach with seashells in her hand, anxious to show him, while Pamela cooled her feet by the water's edge, protecting herself from the raging sun beneath the cover of a straw-brimmed hat.

He reminded himself that no one could ever really be prepared for what this situation entailed, especially here, especially in the cruel world, law, and rule book. The rules of engagement are harsh. You could never get used to brutality—the things you have to accept, the horror behind the door. He shut down the image of Pamela and Chloe; they got deleted like a computer screen scrolling off his mind.

"There is someone else in there; I hear no sound, no one breathing."

Dooley's partner swings the door open. Instantly, a slither of light divides the room in half; two-scale pans of existential justice hang in balance of half-light and half-darkness, two piles of bodies that death weighs equally. The bandits, who have met their destiny, lie bruised and bleeding on the killing floor, alongside the body of a woman with her throat slit ear to ear, her face a contorted danse macabre, another internal struggle for the officers left standing to humanize.

Jeeps and a medical unit are parked all around the garden area. Unlike the city in a metropolitan area, there are no sirens or flashing lights. No gumshoe detectives in wrinkled suits smoking cigarettes; asking questions. The jungle takes care of its own. Brawny men and some women clad in khaki fatigues blend in with crime scene examiners and photographers. Small puddles of blood coagulate in the sandy soil. DNA samples are taken for identification; boot prints decimate the once orderly garden.

Groups of area wildlife clusters were unnoticed from beyond the bush. Curious, they observe the humans perform their communal rituals. Native birds in nearby trees mimic the sounds of clicking from the camera. Chimera monkeys are high in the trees gossiping with hand gestures and sleepy eyes.

A medic steps back as Lenny is being brought into the medical vehicle. She lowers her sunglasses over her eyes and writes something on to her clipboard. Commander Dooley inquires about Lenny's condition.

"He is beaten pretty badly. No broken bones, however, there is a bullet wound incurred during the melee. It seems to have passed through a non-vital part of the abdomen. He will be ok. I administered a sedative. He should sleep for a while. That would be best."

Dooley responds, "All the better. The girl never had a chance. He shouldn't see her that way, brutally raped and throat cut ear to ear."

"What is she to him? Do we know?"

"We suppose a girlfriend, local girl we think. He was not married. I expect the mission will be sending him back to the states as soon as he is able. Pity though, one of my men is collecting his and her belongings. It's a shame he never got to say goodbye."

The medic lowered her head and resumed with her report. Commander Dooley just watched as the last of the body bags were loaded onto the truck.

# AUDITION HALL

A few old metal chairs form a partial row in front of the stage: The orchestra pit is occupied with casting people. Random seats are off to one side where shortlists of performers are waiting in cue to audition.

A thumping jazz track is filling the hall from overhead speakers. Ozzie is performing her part, a momentary interruption from the director calls for a minor change of direction.

Director Silvestre Louis is lean, possessing a statuesque physique, with the elongated muscular structure of an Olympic swimmer. He procures a sweeping hairdo and had been credited over the years for his fashion sense and flamboyant dance routines. He is an up-and-coming choreographer for sure. His chorus lines woo the audience. To his dance troupe, he is stern but fair. He picks his fledglings by hand and shapes them into perfection; however, he has no patience for those who test him, and will promptly deflate an ego or crush a career fantasy with the turn of a phrase. If he ignores you, then consider yourself complemented. If he dismisses you, then you cease to exist in his presence.

"Can we just bring that spotlight to the left a little more? Ozzie, come forward slightly on your left foot when that break comes in. Ok, begin."

A series of extended leg movements ensue. Full-body moves with point stare and pull-away dance sequences. Ozzie's partner comes onto the stage, grabs her in a dominating gesture, and they begin to tango transforming into a Jazz variation. The piece pulls together beautifully. The director is pleased and the troupe looks tired.

In the back of the room by the entrance doors, Nicolette peeps through a smudged window. She is wearing dark glasses so as not to be easily recognized. Her facial reflection is mirrored back at her from between a one-dimensional glass windowpane and the dark refracted lens of her sunglasses; she is separated from herself, as well as from the room on the other side by a thin transparent image of her face. She has branded this dark moment the last association she feels with this estranged place that once was like home to her. Nicolette scans the audition with a cautious eye, as well as a nagging twist in her heart.

Ever since Nicolette vanished from the troupe, giving full notice and no specified reason for leaving, her heart was broken. Each night, she trained with Ozzie coaching and preparing her for the part she was to step into. Helping was her soothing balm, spiritual forgiveness that gave peace. Her life was changing; a baby was coming, and she was not sure what the future was going to be like without Vince. Was he gone? She knew him too well. Aside from his bravado, Vince was not a quitter. To give him space was wise. She had witnessed his unorthodox approach to problem-solving many times. He handled life like a painting. From the chaos, he developed order. However, he needed to be alone to do so, rearranging the elements of a situation, economizing on design, what to leave in and what to take out.

Destiny in its verve sends out agents to beguile and confuse us, mortals. Vince challenged the gods. In painting, if a working composition became trite or irksome, he could abstract it, causing it to work in a whole other universe and forcing the viewers, or in this case, the players, to accept the new rules of perception. She was part of an intricate love story, not a game or a painting. That was one reason Nicolette found life with Vince an irresistible romance.

It is also a reason gifted people possessing great talent, fatigue their loved ones, and irritate others.

Nicolette's reverie was cut short by the clamor and unruly banter rising from the stairwell. Nicolette recognized the boisterous rudeness as Carla and some girls were coming to rehearsal.

Not wanting to be seen, especially by Carla, she walks quickly down the hall to a water fountain. She pretends to be taking a drink as the group comes up the stairs echoing through the corridor. Nevertheless, Carla throws a suspicious glance toward Nicolette's direction, hesitating before she goes in.

Nicolette left the building through the fire staircase; this would lead her to the Wagner street exit out of view from any window she could be spotted from. A brief cloud burst sprinkled the street with rain. She headed back to the apartment.

Off Erie Street by dockside is an old fish market that expands over a whole city block. Small boats as well as large commercial vessels pull into the piers every day bringing deliveries of fresh seafood to the market.

Commercial vans and trucks belonging to chefs and restaurant owners from all over the tri-state area pull up and idle loading their vehicles with seafood and accessories for their week's fare.

The Hole, once a seedy wharf for vagrants and drifters, now grew into a thriving harbor seaport. Some of the brick buildings and warehouses abandoned by failing businesses were being rented out and renovated by galleries and artists of all sorts, bringing a new life and vitality to the beleaguered district.

On the corner wedged into the meatpacking district was the Sand Bar, a landmark for over 100 years. During the day, it serviced curious out-of-towners, while at night, it was a hotbed of activity for the city hipsters on night maneuvers.

When the old man Teddy Debbs took it over from his father, it was a deli, slapping pastrami on rye slinging cold potato pancakes on a plate with hot gravy. Nothing fancy, just your usual grub, greasy spoon specials that stuck to the ribs. Little did Teddy know that when he took over the floundering deli below a flophouse and next to a strip joint, he was going to be the sole proprietor of waterfront real-estate and avant-garde music venue. Not bad for a man who never read a book in his life.

People rarely saw Teddy, the old man. He stayed in his upstairs apartment and chain-smoked cigars all day watching cartoons and western movies. He was dubbed the "the Old Man" by his employees, a loyal gaggle of experienced workers savvy in the deli business, and very much in touch with the local art scene.

Teddy was not that old, he just looked terrible. His suits came from thrift stores, and he never paid more than eight dollars for one. He was extremely cheap; he shaved once a week to save on razors. His skin was like Naugahyde, and so was his upholstery.

Teddy had one obsession with his appearance, and that was his mustache. He fussed over it in between cigars. Besides the deli, his father left him a schnurrbartbinde, more commonly known as a mustache binder. It was an heirloom passed down from the First World War, a man's grooming product of German origin, designed to keep the ends of one's mustache pointed and curled in the fashionable style of Kaiser Wilhelm II. It was made of silk gauze and consisted of two small leather straps and two pieces of metal webbing. You pressed the binder over your entire mustache and attach it to your head, thereby allowing you to train your mustache at home during the day and keep it disciplined while you sleep.

Vincent came up from the wharf studying the sign over the Sand Bar Tavern. The air was loaded with the smell of brine rising from the bay.

An anorexic waitress was standing outside, leaning against a post looking at her cell phone. She immediately recognized Vince.

"Vince, you're back. I haven't seen you for a while."

Vince responds, "Just making a social call."

Girl retorts, "Really? I thought you had me on speed dial. Is your finger broken?"

Vince casts a suspicious eye. "It's been a while. I cleaned up my social register."

She flirts in a way Vince remembers all too well. "Too bad, I get off in an hour if you get restless."

Vince smiles, pushing through the door; he casts a flirtatious wink.

The girl resumes a lax leaning position as she attends her phone.

It is an evening at the Sand Bar and happy hour is about to end. Local characters are drifting about; the music is a mix of light funk with rhythm and blues. People were enjoying tap beer and house wine at half price for the last two hours. The place is a little tipsy. The greasy aromas of French fries and bar food mingle with a waitress wearing too much perfume.

Vince leans into the bar to get the bartender's attention. It is a new guy, Vince doesn't recognize him.

Too many new faces. Once again, Vince gets a vibe of being out of the loop.

In an attempt to shout over the music, Vince asks, "Hey, is Dino working tonight?"

"Yeah, he's in the back."

"Can you ring him, please? Tell him Vince dropped in."

The bartender strolls over to the house phone and rings the kitchen. Vincent leans back looking over the crowd. This could be awhile. Dino cannot always easily get away from the grill, busy kitchen.

The overhead music stops at seven; it's an interlude to the witching hour.

A transvestite piano player takes the stage and begins belting out show tunes, "Mammy, how I Luv ya, how I Luv ya, my dear old Mammy," completely comical.

Semi-drunk people gather around singing. Vince waves to an old friend. Someone over at the piano invites him to join in with a chorus from the cabaret. "Life is cabaret old chums...come to the cabaret." They finish all laughing.

The bartender comes back.

"He said to go to the kitchen."

"Thanks."

Vince finishes his drink and makes his way through the crowd to meet Dino.

The Sand Bar is an outpost for many artists and musicians alike to drop in and out of between gigs and shows. People in the arts hone their craft by osmosis. Places like the Sand Bar are a breeding ground for viruses of the mind. Artists share a kind of kin brotherhood, a psychic support mechanism that develops with understanding—somewhat like the dinner clubs at Princeton and Yale, only without the solid connections, and happy ending success stories.

To the gifted, there is a song going on inside of them, a sweet collaboration of tones, lyrics, and logic, an indulgence that they intuitively channel through each other.

At times, however, as social norms rise and fall, forums like the Sand Bar become the place to go, a pseudo college of Bohemian knowledge, more or less, for want-to-be posers and weekend warriors. Few are capable of holding themselves in the state of listening to their internal songs. They enjoy slumming in the security of a well-established art dive solely for appearance purpose and ego satisfaction. These are the intellectual carpet baggers of our time. At some point, life challenges them with a preordained opportunity to move on and they go.

Vince could always get a kitchen job when things got slow. He was like a carnie working rides every summer on the boardwalk; when the beach closes up for winter, everybody goes home. You have a good time, take your pay, and try to do a painting that sells.

Nicolette having a baby is a game-changer. He is going to have to work later shift hours and push more commercial stuff in the gallery. He knew that was a dead-end, but there is always a way to reinvent. Things could be worse. He could lose Nicci, and that would be bad.

Dino is at the sink, slinking and energetic. He has the slightly built lean frame of a restaurateur, a white tee shirt, and trousers separated by a shiny wide leather black belt. A dry cloth fans out from his back pocket the way stylish men would wear a pocket square in their sports coat. He turns from the sink and greets Vince with a jocular happy smile.

A dish crashes in the background as a tray full of coffee cups rattles on cluttered counter space. The dishwasher is quick to remove large pieces of a broken plate from the floor, tossing them into a large burlap coffee sack that hangs in the middle of the kitchen.

"Pepe, please take it easy. I could build a twenty-foot-high shitter with all the ceramic you guys break around here."

"Look. You see that?"

Dino points to the large burlap bag. He draws Vince's attention to a single dollar bill that is attached to it by a safety pin. Inside the bag are the remains of broken dishes, cups, wine glasses, and so on.

"The old man calls the monument to lost profits."

"He keeps it there as a reminder as to why we don't get raises."

"The old man is still a tightwad, I see," mumbles Vince.

"Worse than ever!" Dino playfully backhands Vince across the chest. "If you ever want to make some extra moola schmoola, you're in. The old man likes ya. Said he misses your Ruebens on garlic bread. We took it off the menu when you left; you made your garlic bread. Man, that's a crowd-pleaser. We tried to substitute commercial stuff. Not the same, man. You gotta part with that recipe. That bread is art, man. Always creamy and warm with melted cheese and garlic. Was that provolone you use?"

"Menchengo. That's all you're getting out of me. If I tell you too much, I'll come in next week and the menu will say Dino's Original Ruben Sengwich," Vince kids him with a mock-accented voice.

"Go ahead; make fun of my aca-cent. You see." They break into a burst of jovial laughter. "What brings you around, Vince?"

"I got some things coming up. I need some cash. I'll drop by next week and talk to the old man."

"Yeah, do that. I'll tell him you stopped by. I will straighten it out with him. Tell me when you wanna start. I take care of it."

They fist bump and hug in neighborhood style.

Vince, not wanting to hold things up in a busy kitchen, turns to get on his way. Dino yells across the porter horn, "Danny daunt charge dis' guy for not-ting he-a wurks here."

It was three days and nights of soul-searching. Foggy and disconcerted Vince picks some lint from his rumpled jacket and straightens his shoulders. He checks his look in the hallway mirror. He will be working at the Sand Bar for an unspecified amount of time; the money is decent, and the hours are flexible. He can still do his art to satisfy his commitment to Damien until his contract folds.

Things are turning around pretty quickly. Three days ago, he saw himself on a looming horizon. An aspiring artist, now he looks in a telling hallway mirror that holds back no truth, unshaved and slovenly, with nowhere to go. Vince holds the handle of the door firmly in his grip. It could have been a suitcase handle or the throttle on his motorcycle that could take him anywhere, but instead, it's the door handle bringing him home.

In the past three days, Vince came to a spiritual intersection in his life that called for a decision—a decision that would determine what kind of man he was, what he could live with, and what he could not. As an artist, he was a creator. As a father, however, could he direct his skills and talents to hold a family together— and what of his family? Who were they? Vince held an alienated idea of who his parents were, shattered and broken up like shards of glass crystallizing the highway after an accident.

His mother, a seamstress, and his father died from black lung at an early age, but not before spawning a son Vincent, in the forgotten inconsequential town in Pennsylvania, where no one ever gets rich or famous.

Umber images pass through the hallway mirror of a small boy with dirt on his face as his mother held up a beautiful hand-made wedding gown she was completing for a neighbor's daughter's wedding.

The lace was brought over from Italy by Crucificia Fantoglia, Vince's mom, who married Michael Galle, an Italian-American soldier stationed in post-war Naples.

His mother had brought with her from Italy the skills of a fine seamstress. Her techniques and knowledge of lace and fine silk were passed on to her from a lost generation of artisans from her small town of Cordon. The boy had with him some charcoal sticks he whittled down from coal shards he found in his Father's corduroy sack. He held up some scribbling on a piece of paper. The mirror gently kissed the image off to Vince, who was deep into the gaze.

Crucificia had always hoped to give birth to a daughter with intentions of making her a wedding gown. Such a romantic notion would be Crucificia's crowning glory to one day have her daughter cherish it as an heirloom legacy to be remembered for generations to come. Such an act would denote Crucificia's and Michael's great love, securing for them a firm legacy in family history.

The drudgery of day-to-day details blurs and distorts over time, mostly forgotten, rarely passed on. It is folklore that endures. This simple wisdom Crucificia held silent in her heart.

She hoarded special lace and embroidery from the shop she worked at in Italy. Her coworkers and local mamma dells wished them well. The priest from St. Peters traveled across the hills on foot to bless the fabrics. A feast ensued; he was fed well. However, in the demanding constraints of rebuilding a post-war America, there was not enough time or money for a second child, Michael, and Crucificia's first and only child was born in the heat of August.

He noticed his mother Crucificia now, outside herself for the first time through this imaginary glow of the mirror. She was not Crucificia as he remembered her at all or his mother, but a radiant transformation of love. The materials she held in her ghostly hands were soft and iridescent.

He came from a culture of life. Life was embraced. Sacrifice is what people did in his parent's guardian world. Life was instilled in his heart. However, in the world he would come to know growing up, it could be just as easily recklessly abandoned.

Nicolette was on the fire escape feeding Tramp when Vince entered the room. He watched her from the doorway, he was searching for the right words to say. Tramp slipped back toward the window. Vince drew near to her. Nicolette stood silent.

Vince whispers in her ear, "I guess everyone is a little restless and can't sleep."

No answer from Nicci. Tramp hops the railing and disappears behind the building.

"I was thinking about what you said the other night, about how you're not a little girl anymore, I guess I have to man up on some stuff myself. I wasn't thinking clearly. I said some things. I love you Nicci. I want what you want. I'm not afraid anymore."

# PART TWO

Sonia, Sonia, Sonia—pretty and pleasingly plump, as Mom always said—always the bridesmaid, never the bride. The older daughter who always keeps her ears open and her mouth shut loaded with textbook knowledge and afternoon talk show wisdom always knows the courtroom drama outcomes before any of the television judges can pass a verdict.

In a flowered dress, she is a mountain paradise complete with hills and valleys. With her hair pulled back, she has the soft face of the messenger of goodwill depiction one might find on a tarot card. Her heart is always in the right place; however, a few curves around her mid-section may be meandering in the wrong direction, not adding to her voluptuousness, but rather contributing to large sedentary settlements around the waistline and buttocks. At the end of the day, however, it is not physical chubbiness that sends potential suitors away, but her doting attention to her mother's needs. Sonia: the consummate mamma's girl, the matron handmaiden, and a lady in waiting.

There was the incident with Jean-Paul, the Costa Rican gentleman who pursued her for a full year. They dated. He showered her with perfume and gifts of candy and flowers; he was mad for her, writing her poetry professing his passion, but, again, the constant caring for her mother became too much for him to bear. He went away, sadly realizing that even if her mother were to drop dead tomorrow, Sonia would still put the memory of her mother's decomposing body before his needs.

She was also modest and shy, reluctant to get naked before men. She would hang her large white underwear on a drying rack after laundry, secretly resenting them.

"When the right man comes along, will you be ready?" her mother would ask her.

Friday afternoons were good days to shop on the Avenue. The weekend sales bring out the bargain hunters for first picks at the newly presented items.

Sonia and Mother are occupied throwing baby clothes all around the sale table with other women seeking the first come first serve goods. The store manager exchanges banter with a security guard before stepping into his office.

Nicolette stands off to the side, watching in disbelief and a little embarrassed as her sister and mother fling items around in frenzy.

This kind of behavior was new to her; she was not used to this very different lifestyle. Sonia somehow could fit in with her mother's generation, swallowing all that old-world culture pap. It somehow complemented her older sister's lethargic standard of living; Nicolette was uncomfortable in it.

Nicolette, however, even though raised and brought up the same as Sonia, never wanted to become part of the cut-rate urban subculture that prevailed around her. Young women pushing baby carriages, growing old before their time, hanging out with their mother, never fit the bill for her.

Having detached from mother-daughter stuff early in her formative years, Nicolette embraced instead the new generation attitude. She reached for glamour and independence from old-world culture and values. Nicolette turned inward escaping the suffocating tentacles of the little world that constantly tried to snare her.

Nicolette held no desire to mix and mingle; she craved a modern lifestyle free from trite connotation. It was through dance she was equal to do what she wanted without stereotypes. Through her talent and hard work, she could cross barriers, bringing her outside the small confines of a strict frightened culture that insulated, keeping you small, as it did for Sonia.

Nicolette wanted to embrace all that her generation could offer her. She knew she could do it through dancing, but now, baby clothes at the bargain store; Sonia, wearing that loud tight-fitting flowered dress, and last but not the least, her mother was old and dressed old. Nicolette saw herself quite differently.

A glinting moment of clarity flashed through her mind, frightening her. She had no word for it, but the word was conformity.

Was she being sucked into the black hole of silent desperation? She went blank, a dull confusion was circulating inside her.

Nicolette, having had weeks of this behavior, is beginning to show weariness from the pregnancy and the over excitement of mother and sister tossing things upside down talking fast half English half Spanish. She was feeling isolated, unable to share their excitement. She walked to the window of an ice cream shop. Spying a side view, she became uncomfortable with her unfamiliar reflection, the increasing tummy bulge. She thought to herself a grim proclamation, "I may as well have a sign on my back saying, 'Look at me ladies, I joined the club. I am one of, you know, I'm preggers. Ok, come let us all be one happy family.'"

Reality hit home in one clear second.

She has become what millions of women had become since the beginning of the human race: pregnant.

Nicolette said to Sonia, "I am going to get an ice cream cone. I will wait for you across the street. Meet me there when you two are finished." She turned leaving Sonia and Mom to their shopping.

Waiting until Nicolette was clearly out of earshot, Sonia pulls close to Mother. "I am so glad the ultrasound said it's a girl." She picks up an article of clothing and fingers through it.

"Oh, that's cute," she interrupted holding up a tiny garment.

"I would much rather help her with a girl. It will be easier on you too, mama."

Mother poignantly responds, "Let me tell you something. Vince will be working at that restaurant all night. Your sister thinks she is going to start dancing right away. Well, I got news for them both. I am no babysitter! She had better marry him before he figures out he can't afford her tastes and leaves her."

Sonia responds, "She told me Vince wants to marry her. It's Nicci, Mamma. She is a stubborn one."

Sonia casts a sideward glance over at Nicolette, who is sitting on a bench eating an ice cream cone admiring her stiletto heel boots, a combination of images that do not compliment the demeanor of a burgeoning pregnant woman.

"Look at her over there. She is eating that ice cream cone like a little kid. Like she just cannot wait for this to all blow over. We should get some sneakers or something. She looks like a hoochie mamma with those wild clothes."

"She will not wear what we buy her, Sonia. She was always a very stubborn child. Nothing gets in her way. Remember the time when your father took you and her to the carnival? And Nicolette wanted to go on that carousel? Your father told her no so many times. Then, as soon as it slowed down, she tried to jump on it and got thrown off. The man was yelling at your father for not watching his kid. Your father told me that even though she scraped her knee very badly, and he gave her a stern tongue-lashing. He held her hand any time we were ever around a carousel again. He said he could see in her eyes that if she got the chance to jump that carousel again, she would do it. That is Nicolette."

The neon letter (S) on the Sand Bar was faulty, causing it to flash with no particular rhythm. The flickering added a carnival-like tackiness to the display. In the early afternoon, the bar was open for a few hours concerning the ironworkers and trade people who still dropped in to take the edge off before going home. It closed for a few hours and reopened at eight o'clock P.M. to usher in the cavalcade of marauders on their Vampire run through the underground circuit of artsy happenings and garage band rock shows.

Typical nights at the club presented a line of people stylishly dressed and ready to star out. It was not unusual for young trendy designer students to alter wedding dresses or vintage clothes posing as human mannequins making statements on fashion or trending some up to the minute avant-garde idea.

A good mix of music is usually playing loud. Disco lights and all sorts of bells and whistles are distracting anyone from any level of deep conversation. Most sentences are reduced to word bytes of only a few characters. More futuristic conversationalists found it easier to text on their mobile devices rather than talk with the person sitting next to them, freeing them from the strain of attempting to speak.

Once inside, people from all different backgrounds are dancing in exaggerated and bizarre dance steps modish to the times; chic trendy types line up along the bar.

Cell phone selfies are all the rage. The selfie stick replaced the disposable camera.

Back in the kitchen, Vince is flipping burgers on the grill. Dino is telling jokes.

Vince looks out through a spy hole, order window, to recognize a celebrity artist in the crowd with an entourage around him. He observes with curiosity.

A man in a shabby suit takes the stage, telling jokes.

On the other side of the room, a handsomely well-dressed conservative-looking man stands out at the celebrity table.

Vince, still watching from the kitchen, is fascinated by the pomp and circumstance that is happening before him.

Someone at the celebrity table makes an awkward move, knocking something over, spilling it on the quirky celeb.

The personality guest begins a tantrum of stamping his foot flaunting embarrassment. He whispers something to his valet, insisting to leave. The entourage escorts him out to a waiting car.

The man in the suit is standing with the maître 'de and the waiter, handing him a wad of cash, hurriedly. After paying the bill, he scuttles toward the door.

From out of the crowd, a newspaperman emerges with a camera and begins asking the suited man questions following him, while other paparazzi appear from out of nowhere taking pictures. Some were recognized as local media hounds, others just local hacks trying to get the scoop for the late-night edition.

Bouncers get between the journalist and the suited man who makes his escape through the door and is gone.

Vince watches on at the melee with a look of interest.

Dino notices that Vince is not paying any attention to the grill orders, and comes over to help. Vince is completely preoccupied with the kitchen portal.

Vince blurts out, "I just saw Basil Limier and Maxwell Kidd being escorted out by our bouncers. What's going on?"

"Yeah, yeah. Table 12. They have that table reserved. They are like moviemakers or something. They come in about once a month or so, usually to celebrate something. You know them?"

Vince responds, "I heard about them. Limier is a gallery big wig, and Max Kidd is the video artist he handles."

Dino adds, "Something like that, that guy Kidd, the tall pasty one has, how you say, a...loft parties that get him in the papers all the time. One night, they bring this crazy old woman in here all dressed up like some kind of voodoo queen or some-ting like dis'. She had with her a gold-painted peacock, a wild-looking ting, with this beautiful tail and all. It looked like a gay rooster. The old man made her take it outside as it kept shittin' on the dance floor. These big long green stronz, and peoples was slippin' on it." Dino laughs at the absurdity of it while Vince hoists a batch of chicken tenders from the deep fry basket.

An order for a burger and fries came in from a server. Vince grabbed it from the order line. He threw a burger on the grill and just started frying it. Dino sliced potato into some steak fry cuts and tossed them in a separate deep fry basket. Both men just watched the basket submerge into the boiling golden oil. Greasy bubbles rose from the bottom of the fryer, slowly thudding to the surface and exploding with a hot and sticky pop.

Dino gazed lovingly into the golden foam, "B'utiful, ain't it?"

A sleepy cadmium yellow sun pushes its crowned head through the thinning sheet of the morning fog, causing a stratum haze. Old Mr. Sunshine blinked just long enough to assure morning commuters the status quo is alive and well along the Hudson Parkway. Sunglasses and designer eyewear conceal the salt waterlogged eyes of daily commuters. Irritated, weary travelers jockey for position to get to work before the big bell rings.

Vince exited to a more scenic route that would take him along the suburban side road. Sprawling fields of apple orchards and meadows complete the landscape. It was a quiet escape for him after a tedious working week in the kitchen.

He takes the road to a high bluff that overlooks a natural rock formation with some twisted trees and water views. Far off over the horizon, a thin glimpse of the parkway divides the sky, diamond caps, and sunbeams bounce from car to car in perfect metered time.

Vince parks at a grassy rest area. He reaches to the back of the cycle and pulls a travel bag from a rack along with a large pad and some chalks.

Making his way to a clearing, he momentarily rested by a stony cliff, searching out cloud formations and scenery thinking all the while how much closer the huge rolling billows seemed to appear further up the precipice-urging his ascent. So immeasurable and large was the sky, an inverted ocean he imagined, where the clouds are like waves touching down over the horizon brought forward by a turquoise blue-green sky both vast and infinite. How easy childlike phenomena can be explained on a visual level without the hodgepodge of physical science and intricacies.

As he is sketching, the forms begin to take on images of shapes and faces. He can make out branches that look like arms and cloud formations that take on angelic likeness.

Two women are having a picnic not too far from him; they entertain a small boy playing in the grass, and one of the women throws down a blanket. Thinking he was alone, Vince was distracted by the sound of voices. He could not help watching them in their simple natural state, cutting bread, tending to the child, leisurely and at ease, sharing simple conversation; a ballet-like rhythm possessed them unequal to anything in compulsory time. Automatically, Vince began to sketch them.

In the outside world, we tend to clutter. The inner soul has a divine simplicity spectacle over the mind where past, present, and future tend to merge. A sky is a form of the ocean, and the ocean a form of the sky. Vince looked over at the thin horizon at the orderly traffic moving the lives therein.

One of the women becomes aware that Vince is drawing them; she fixes her hair and straightens her back, whispering over to the other woman who giggles and feigns not to look.

After some drawing, Vince packs up his things and loads them onto the cycle. He tears a page from the pad. Walking over to them, Vince hands a drawing to the woman, presumably the child's mother. It is about the boy playing. "Ladies, a remembrance of your day," he chides. Vince walks back to his cycle, starts up, and heads away.

It is a tired, peaceful evening. She is glad to have Vince back at the apartment again. Nicolette surfs between the latest talent shows and ballroom dancing specials on the TV. A shapely dancer glides across the screen taking the hand of her partner. Together, they begin moving their feet in matching rhythm to the quickstep. Nicolette is lying on the couch in her pajamas eating potato chips. She feels a bump in her stomach.

She gets up and hurries into the bathroom. A stream of warm liquid runs down along her legs, soaking her. She suspects that her water has broken and panics. Unsure of what to do first, she runs to the phone and calls her mother.

Marcella Sanchez Castro has a name in full, although, besides local junk mail, it has been some time since anyone has addressed her by it. She comfortably resigned to the title of Mommy, Ma, or Mother Dearest, the latter being reserved for more sarcastic moments from anxious daughters.

This evening, Mother sits by the table leafing through a healthy living catalog noticing pairs of premium footpad inserts for her shoes. Her feet have been aching for a while, and she recently discussed with Sonia about purchasing them for herself. These are small comforts Mother sometimes treats herself to when spare funds allow. Daughter Sonia was looking over her shoulder, eyeing comfy, casual Capris that shared the same page.

The phone rings, breaking the silence. Mother shakes her head in a predictable huff, hoping it was her friend Stella, the local gossip with a good story.

"Hello?"

"Mamma! I think the water thing broke."

The mother responds, "Oh my God, it's ok, baby. I will get Sonia, and we will be right there."

Sonia, still looking over her mother's shoulder, answers, "What? Oh my God. I am right here."

Mother says, "Ok. I will tell Vince."


Nicolette stares nervously at her cell phone, retrieving Vince's number to dial. She waits. From under a pile of the clutter accumulated on the kitchen table, Nicolette can hear Vincent's phone ringing and vibrate under a stack of junk mail. Nicolette realizes Sonia is dialing Vincent.

"Oh, shit. Nice, Vince," Nicolette spews profanities into the air.

She pushes the mail aside to get to Vincent's phone. A letter from Sierra Narvon falls to the floor. In her haste, Nicolette slides over it with her foot pushing it under the radiator vent. Nicolette grabs Vincent's phone and puts it into her bag. She begins packing her bag for the hospital in a hastened rush.

The letter purloined behind the radiator vent extended about one-quarter of an inch onto the floor. It is a written statement from authorities of Serria Narvon informing Vince about the tragedy that befell Lenny Paxton. The letter shows a return address for Lenny. However, it will go unnoticed for quite some time.

A lone taxi rolls up to the apartment building. Sonia tells the cabbie the situation, while Mother climbs the stairwell leading to Nicolette's apartment.

"My mother will be right down with my sister."

"Do you need a hand getting her?"

"No. We can manage. Thanks anyway."

Sonia closes the door and heads into the building.

When they come back out, all three squeeze into the back seat of Clyde Odell's Crown Victoria cab. Nicolette is sandwiched in the middle. Clyde scuttles out and places the luggage into the trunk.

As the taxi rumbles to its destination, Mother breaks into the loose chatter. "Nicolette. Where is Vince? Did you call him?"

Nicolette responds, "He forgot his phone. Oh my God. Before I forget, here, Sonia. Take this phone and give it to Vince when he comes back to the apartment."

The mother goes off on a tirade, "When he comes back here? What is he going to do in the apartment? He should be with you!"

"Ma, he doesn't know where I am. I can't call him. I think he is at the gallery talking with Damien."

"Sonia could meet him at the apartment and they can come back together," Mother is now talking to the side of Nicolette's face. Nicolette is staring straight ahead holding her stomach. "You two are like a couple of children. Who is going to raise this baby? When I was your age, I was doing everything myself. Your father was useless already, drunk every day, that bum. You better get married or you are going to wind up like me."

Sonia chimes in, talking to the other side of Nicolette's face, "Mamma. Not now. Her water just broke. You're making us crazy."

Mother, still talking, "Crazy? You would have been crazy a long time ago if it wasn't for me, working like I had to do. No time to play all day like you kids, drawing pictures and dancing." Mother points to the parking lot of the hospital and shouts to Sonia, "Tell him to drive in here."

The cabbie turns into the lot without any further direction from Sonia.

The cabbie Clyde Odell lifts his baggy eyelids to the rearview mirror where he can better communicate to Sonia.

"Hey, should I pull into the emergency room spot?"

"Yes, that would be fine."

The taxi turns around to circle the lot and pulls up to the emergency room entrance; Clyde gets out and helps all three out of the cab. An orderly comes out to assist them. He brings a wheelchair for Nicolette. Mother wheels her in. The orderly is chasing behind her. Sonia comes back out and gets into the taxi, telling Clyde to bring her back to the apartment where he picked them up.

Damien's office and gallery are on the ground floor of a converted car garage and storage facility. It is nestled in the trendy downtown quarter known as the Gannon district. Until recently, the Gannon section of town was a forsaken heap of abandoned buildings and old brick factories. Recently, however, creative entrepreneurs, restaurants, artists, and housing developers all seized on the opportunity to utilize the abandoned classic architecture turning it around to the advantage of alternative lifestyle types who preferred to carve out a niche for themselves away from Main Street.

It was here that Vincent Galle was called to meeting with Damien and a few board consultants concerning his new approach in art design.

In light of the changes that Vincent has been going through, he has been examining his own life and soul, recording his experiences in paint and expression. He has been experimenting with the undercurrent of the art ideal that has been questioning artists since the beginning of art itself. What good does art do? If I am welcomed and paid by patrons for the sake of their enjoyment, then my product is amusement, he thought to himself. If I desire to communicate a legacy, well then, the art community has a subtle, unconscious, refining influence that must be dealt with. The creative process teaches the artist to play as a child does. Life, on the other hand, requires those games to be disciplined and mature at the end of the day. This maddening divide in mental preferences does not play easily to a creative artist with a newborn child on the way.

God stands vigilant at the roulette table of free will making sure no one cheats.

From the soft chalk office walls, the dull echo of conversation resonated. On the floor, proofs of paintings and prints lie in piles. A computer screen mounted on the wall displayed images of new paintings some in-studio, not even dry.

Damien is leaning over some prints of Christ and Mary Madeleine. Slightly lifting his head, Damien shifts his eyes to Vince with a smug glare.

"Vince, I do not care if she was seconds from being stoned to death for being a harlot or anointed woman of the year. The new idea of yours is not working. Vincent, flying cherubs, saints. This is a contemporary gallery, not the Vatican."

"Seriously, Damien. You are treating me like a windup doll. We have a contract."

"Here, look at this, Vincent. A Madonna on a cell phone nursing a baby. Nobody can hang that on their wall. Your patrons come to see your design work, Vincent, big broad color fields, the blending pastel shades you do so well. They won't hang this in their apartments with its dark medieval religious hetero. They cannot relate."

"They can't or you can't?"

"We worked together for a long time, Vincent. I consider you my friend. That was not necessary."

I am sorry, I didn't mean that. I just feel very strongly about these new paintings. It's my life, Damien, my work."

Damien hangs his head poignantly over the prints. He looks up coldly stating.

"Our patrons do not want to be reminded of their sins. They want to forget them. That's what selling art is all about. It's wine and chocolate and visual pleasures to comfort and distract. Opiate for the guilt-ridden."

Vince begins gathering his prints. Damien's cell phone rings. Damien snatches it from the table; checking the readout, he pushes it against his chest. In an exasperated sigh, he says,

"Vincent, I have to take this call. You can leave these. Stop by next week, but take them next week. I do not want them hanging around. They give me the creeps. I might have something coming up for that biannual show. Get cracking on some new designs. Ciao ciao."

Vince rambles over to the victory coffee shop; some tables were set outside partially filled with perky couples and a few mom and daughter acts peppered in to add a sense of community to an otherwise pretentious street lined with galleries and show-offs. Hipster chicks were dressed in black plaids, shouting with statement tattoos from across the Hudson. On a table was a tattered paperback of the Illustrated Man, a classic Bradbury novel, about a collection of eighteen startling visions of humankind's destiny, unfolding across a canvas of decorated skin. So began the plot summary by Stig O'Hara.

Vincent stands outside a coffee shop holding his coffee. Looking around, he inhales a deep breath. Walking might be the best thing to do right now. He reasons silently and begins to head across the Avenue. A small white delivery truck whizzes by him, catching his attention. On the back and sides was a monogram in gold and green. Scribbled in a gothic font ironically tattoo-like was the inscription DYLAN WELLES GALLERY.

He watched it turn into the Welles Gallery loading area. A sleek woman stepped out from the doorway, barking directions at the driver. A lanky man comes forward from behind a garage door dressed in white painter overalls wearing a paperwhite cap the kind maintenance personnel wear. He is joined by two other men from the gallery. The lanky man opens the truck door and they begin unloading long tall cartons onto dollies and move them into the gallery.

The woman stood poised like a reed, her black hair shining in the sun. Whether imagined or not, Vince thought for a moment that he could smell leather and citral emanating from her direction. A blue thread of cigarette smoke encircled her. Vince could not hear it, but her cell phone must have been ringing because she quickly glanced at it and took the call. The last thing Vince could notice was how she put out her cigarette; she took one last puff, dropped it to the ground, and crushed it underfoot before disappearing through the doorway.

After a few moments of mild detachment from his immediate surroundings, Vince realized he should be checking in with Nicolette.

Rummaging through his clothes, he realized he forgot his phone. He hurried back to the apartment.

Vincent opens door to the apartment and was shocked to hell to find Sonia sitting in a chair eating a sandwich with the television on.

Sonia jumps up out of the chair hysterically waving her hand and wiping her mouth with a napkin.

"Vince, we have been looking all over for you. Thank God, you came right back. We have to go! We have to leave right now." Sonia reaches into her bag and hands Vince his cell phone. "Here. You forgot your cell phone. Oh my God."

Vince in a state of decompression asks, "Sonia, what happened?"

"The water broke. Nicolette is with Mom at the hospital. I came back to get you, Vince. C'mon, we have to go. Oh my God!"

"Ok, Sonia. Calm down and get everything we need."

Sonia replies, "Ok, it's all in this bag. I will call a taxi."

Vince tells her, "Sonia, are you kidding me? C'mon, let's go. You can eat that on the way." Vince grabs Sonia's arm and starts to lead her to the door.

Sonia is protesting as Vince is practically dragging her down the hallway. Despite Sonia's exaggerated hysterical sounds, Vince manages to get her through the exit door and onto the street.

Vince is standing in front of his motorcycle with Sonia. He hands her the helmet.

"Here, put this on," Vince commands her.

"What? This? No way. Oh no. I am not going on that thing. I'm too big. I'll call a cab and meet you."

"Sonia, this is quicker. You will be safe. C'mon. This little engine can pull a lot of weight."

Sonia is struggling in her dress attempting to mount the seat, "Vince, I can't get my leg up. It's my dress!" Sonia struggles with her tight dress. She is heavy, to begin with. Vince hunches over trying to help her.

"Jeez, Sonia. Get your big ass up there."

"It's not me, Vince. The dress is too tight."

Vince, getting exasperated, takes the dress by the seam, giving a quick tug, splitting her dress along the side ridge causing Sonia to shriek as if in pain. Still making hysterical squeaking noises, Sonia finally mounts the cycle.

Vincent, in an agile leap, mounts the cycle turning the throttle, starting the machine. Together, they race through the alley on to the street.

Sonia looks cartoonish and large but comfortable from the back. Hitting cans, bumps, and puddles, debris splashes around Sonia's ankles. She pulls her lips into a visage of distress, continuing to utter expletives and curses. Vince gently adjusts to the numbing muffled hum inside his helmet the gentle mantra calling him to destiny.

Mother, Sonia, and Vince are nervously gathered in the waiting room of the Friends of Mercy Medical Center waiting to hear from the doctor handling Nicolette's delivery. The cabbie that was unable to resist the drama sacrificed a few fares just to witness what the turnout was going to be like. He purchased some donuts and coffee and was now chatting with Sonia, regaining her composure from the ride with Vince.

A young nurse enters the room to inform them that Nicolette is very close to her time. Another nurse with a thick Haitian accent enters the room, holding surgical scrubs and a face mask. She approaches Vince in a very matter-of-fact way, directing him to the room where he can prepare to witness the birth. Vince looks over into a doorway where nurses and the doctor are discussing the procedure.

Sonia is spread out on a chair being looked over by an intern. Mother is wiping Sonia's brow with a damp cloth. Vincent peers through a door where Nicolette is being attended to. She sees Vince and weakly raises her hand in a gesture to wave him in.

The large nurse with the Haitian accent descended on Vincent.

"Hello, are you Vincent? I am Jillian Wrens. Head nurse here looking over Nicolette. She requested that you witness the birth. Are you ready?"

Vincent is caught off guard and responded, "Ready?"

"You are going to see your baby being born, aren't you?"

"You mean I'm not staying out here? I'm going in there?"

"Yes, yes. Don't be nervous. You're not squeamish, I hope."

"No, no. I'm ok."

"Ok, then let's get on with it. Nature is calling, you know."

The nurse escorted Vince into a changing room.

"Hurry. There is not much time. I will bring you in when you are ready." The nurse handed Vince a pile of hospital clothing and shut the door on him.

Sonia and Mother are patiently sitting in the waiting room of the maternity ward. Pale mint walls surround them. A light scent of a medical institution filled the room as an overhead vent pushed clear air down and onto mother and daughter.

Sonia lifted a light sweater, pulling it over her shoulder complaining the vent in the waiting room was too much on her; yet physically moving would be too much of an imposition on her already overtaxed comfort zone.

The clock on the wall slowly twisted from 6:45 to 8:45. Opening and closing doors were the only action for 2 hours. Nurses and interns pass each other with little more than a swift acknowledgment. Both ladies gave little thought to their surroundings nodding gently in and out of naps. A nurse came into the waiting room. She was a different nurse from before, asking the women if they would like to see the baby girl. The women energetically rose and together, they walked along the corridor to a large windowed room where Nicolette was brought for recovery.

Vince was leaning over Nicolette, holding her hand and touching her face. Between them, a newborn child was asleep in Nicci's arms. She was pink and blotchy and heavy with sleep. Behind little slits, glassy eyes were coming awake experiencing a new world outside the womb, free from the umbilical cord with vital organs all functioning independently.

Time is moving forward. People already present in this life change like the seasons. Public service workers check schedules.

Watchmen and postal workers punch their clocks. The candy corn Sun and giggle belly Moon play hide and seek while fate plays the numbers game.

The struggle for the apartment and bills that have become due are not so great or inescapable. Things are rolling along but sacrifices must be made.


Responsibility and punctuality is not a trait best reserved for the artistic, however, long hours of concentration and flexible endurance are traits most artists are gifted with. Focusing passion back and forth from child to career is a rhythm similar to a brushstroke. Little sleep and adrenaline can test you. You can get your second wind or you can burn out, but either way, you cannot give up. Boxers can get knocked down after a few solid rounds of punishing blows, but it is the champion that remains standing who comes back. A professional fighter cannot go into the ring halfhearted.

Nicolette is walking the floor at 2:35 A.M. Agitated and pacing, Vince is drawing at his easel, sketching a design for Damien. He has been selling well at the gallery although he hates the conformity his work has taken on. His schedule at the Sand Bar is afternoons tonight. He then returns home to paint until sunrise, leaving him just enough time to help Nicolette, thus salvaging himself about 3 hours of sleep. That is just enough; any more would be wasting valuable time.

Nicolette, on the other hand, is not coping so well with her new lifestyle. The cuteness of the baby soon wore off and the responsibility of a dependent human being is beginning to take its toll on her once self-indulgent life.

For about a month, she showed the baby off as most new moms are proud to do. Everyone fussed. There never seemed to be enough diapers, and two women under the same roof at any age is never easy.

"I don't know what to do. This kid cries all night. She hates me. I know this baby hates me. My mother always used to tell us that two women under the same roof could not coexist. Now I know what this means."

"You had three under the same roof," mentioned Vince.

Nicolette cast a fish eye over to Vince's direction blasting him. "We would have been better off with a boy. I can't take this. She is already a bitch."

Vince answers in almost a too passive-aggressive tone to be believable.

"Nic, you should not talk like that. She's just a baby. Be nice to her daddy's little angel. Here, give her to me. Now, princess, don't cry. Here, help daddy draw. See how nice. See, she stopped crying. She just wants to play."

Nicolette is looking at Vince with jealousy and contempt. She displays uneasiness when he and the baby are together. As the two of them get on quite well, Nicolette is feeling left out. She is beginning to show crankiness and signs of postpartum depression. She cries at the tip of a hat and has lost her sense of humor.

Nicolette calmly walked over to Vince and handed him the baby, then walked to the window where Tramp was perched out front. Shushing him away, she stares out the window declaring.

"Vince, I am going to jump out this fucking window."

"Oh, don't do that Nic. You could hurt yourself on the fire escape."

Nicolette did not appreciate his sarcastic humor, not at 2:30 in the morning, and not when she is crying out for help. Nicolette picked up a paper towel roll from the counter motioning toward Vince in a threatening way, growling.

"Grrraaa! Uhhh!"

Then, throwing the roll into the sink, she ran off into the bedroom, locked the door, and cried herself to sleep.

Vince stayed late at the Sand Bar this evening, picking up some overtime due to an employee call-out and a busy crowd. It is closing time and later than usual for Vince.

The staff is cleaning up and horsing around. Dino is passing bottles of beer out to everyone. A few waitresses are sitting on the counter talking about going to a concert and hoping to make enough money in tips to cover it. The Sassy 5 foot two eyes of blue, all of a young nineteen, rants on about her concert tickets, and how crummy tips are going to mess up her plans.

Some others are going about dividing the evening's gratuities. Dino is scrubbing down the grill. A dishwasher takes some discarded food and scraps it into a Styrofoam container. He proceeds to take out the trash. Two dishwashers drag garbage bags to the dumpster. A bum is grubbing leftovers. One of the dishwashers hands him some Styrofoam containers with French fries along with a few return orders. They exchange some jumbled dialogue and go their ways.

Vincent is putting broken dishes into the old man's monument, a burlap bag that hangs from the ceiling. Out of monotony, Vince starts piecing together their shapes. Looking at them and reconfiguring each one, sassy five-foot-two eyes of blue approaches, taking a perfectly formed crescent-shaped pie dish out of his hand and holds it over her head like a Tierra, waltzing around Vince mimicking a poem.

"I am the princess of the steeple. I serve all the pretty people drinking and thinking that they got it made." She then curtseys in mock fashion tossing the dish into the sack.

Vince studies her with interest.

Vince takes her by the shoulders and leads her under a picture frame that is hanging on the wall.

She strikes a pose as if she is the painting. Vince lifts her hand and poses her with a plate behind her head like a halo. The theme of halos and saints are some ideas he has been experimenting with since he rode to the cliffs, an inspirational awakening has sparked in him since the baby was born.

"Now, you are the saint of the Sand Bar kitchen," Vince proclaims.

The waitress walks over to the specials board displaying the menu of the day and wipes it clean.

She hands Vincent a piece of chalk and challenges him, "Immortalize me."

Vincent takes the chalk from her hand and begins to sketch her. The staff gathered around him.

He does an eerie likeness of a saint-type character.

Unbeknownst to the oblivious kitchen staff, a sleek sedan had parked outside the Sandbar around the back-delivery entrance. A fashionable gentleman made his way over misplaced cobblestones and fallen dumpster trash, paying little mind to the mess splashing on his Italian shoes.

Basil Lanier was on the route this evening to make a reservation for a gathering for his client. He was waiting for the Sand Bar to close to the public, then he would sneak in the service door and make his arrangements with the manager on hand. He could not take the chance of being spotted by the press or paparazzi, for fear of having them show up and causing a social fiasco for him and his celebrity artist, who in this case has a phobic fear of the public and must be treated with the utmost assurance that no chance of scandal will take place.

As Basil Lanier was approaching the service entrance, he caught himself in the middle of a fascinating happening.

He watched with serendipity as Vince was producing a type of performance art in the most unlikely of ordinary places. The room, the pieces, the subject matter were all falling into place remarkably in a scheme to something he had been discussing with his associate Dylan Welles, the art tycoon.

Basil Lanier, art consultant extraordinaire, talent scout, and all-around fetch-it-boy for all things concerning Dylan Welles, had serendipitously discussed at a meeting that prior week to search for something dynamic and contemporary for the gallery. A streak of new "spiritualism" was the term used to find an artist that can spark a fresh dynamic was his mission.

Basil, being astute and somewhat intuitive, had a good vibe about what he was observing. He recognized Vince as someone he has seen before but could not place his work. This, however, is a rare synchronistic discovery that sometimes happens in art, a situation where opportunity and product join together like atoms attracting in a quantum universe to form a new element. In laymen's terms, those of us experiencing these emotions in day to day life might refer to it as love at first sight.

Basil Lanier silently observed as Vince completed the piece; another staff person noticed the stranger by the door and acknowledged, "Hey, Mister. You shouldn't be here. We are closing."

Dino, immediately identifying the stranger, a Basil Lanier quickly stepped in.

"Oh no, it's ok, Deb. Mr. Lanier has some business. Sorry to keep you waiting Mr. Lanier. The maitra'de has gone home, but she left word with me. I can take the information. I'll make sure she gets it tomorrow."

"Sure, sure, of course. Not a problem. I would phone my reservation in as I have done in the past; however, in light of our last event Faux Pas, I would much rather do it this way. I am glad you understand. Forgive me if I might change the subject, I am noticing this sketch here. You have some work at the Prince Gallery, I believe."

Basil was addressing to Vincent but seemed to be talking to the drawing on the message board.

Vince, a bit surprised by the acclamation, "Yes."

Basil, not smiling, but looking pleased, asks, "Will you sell me that right now? What do you want for it?"

Vince was not sure how to respond, he answered with the first thought that came into his head, "Well it's not my blackboard."

Basil, familiar with the awe he can impose on new artists that recognize him, turned up the volume to gentle and avuncular.

"I have an associate that might be very interested in this. Would you take two hundred dollars for it? it is what I have in cash on me. I can write you a check. Or you can visit me tomorrow at the gallery; I am hoping you will do that anyway. Oh, don't worry about the board. I can have it replaced tomorrow well before the club opens."

Vince asks Dino as if asking a parent's permission.

"Is it ok, Dino? With the board, I mean?"

Dino nods dumbfounded.

Vince settles, "Ok. Two hundred would be fine."

Basil, always happy to make a deal, chants, "Good, good. Oh dear, I hope it doesn't smudge. Can I wrap it in butcher paper or something?"

Vince snapping into reality, responds, "Oh, not to worry, hold one second. Does anyone have hairspray, in your bag, locker, anywhere?"

"Yeah, I do."

Sassy five-foot-two eyes of blue reaches into her bag retrieving a large can of Hairnet Ultra Hold, handing it to Vince.

Vince shakes the can then proceeds lightly spraying the chalkboard, "That should do it. It won't smudge."

Vincent removes the board from the wall and hands it to Basil. Basil hands him the money and a business card, instructing him to come by the gallery.

Basil, reflecting on Dino, says, "I will call in tomorrow for the reservation. See you tomorrow, Vincent."

Vincent stands thunderstruck holding the money and the hairspray. He hands the server back her can of hairspray and pushes some money into her hand.

Five–foot-two eyes of blue looks at the cash in her hand. It was more than enough to cover the concert.

"Wow, thanks. What's this for?"

"A tip, I guess. Enjoy the concert."

Everyone silently listened as the sedan pulled away crushing debris and shaking cobblestones loose in its wake.

The apartment has a dull quiet around it, heavy exhaustion like ether might produce, or the peace incurred the morning after the last canon was fired on the battlefield. Nicolette is sleeping in bed. Vince is nodding sitting up on a chair with the baby in his arms. Vince's cell phone starts ringing on the cushion next to his head, waking up the baby. Nicolette just fell asleep and is rustling to the sound. Vince jumps up and puts the baby back in the crib; he examines the phone and takes the call from Damien.

"Hello, Damien. What's up?"

Damien answers bright and chipper, not a hint in his voice that it is somewhere around four o'clock in the morning, "I'm sorry Vince. I hope I'm not waking you. Something has come up. Can you come to the gallery this afternoon?"

"Sure. What is it? Is everything alright?"

Damien, still sounding like the morning magpie, "Can you come in now? I'll see you in a little while."

Vince in half a dream state asks, "What is going on?"

Damien slowly slipping into drama mode mentions, "I just had a visit from Basil Lanier. He had someone with him. Dylan Welles, have you heard of her?"

Vince suddenly awakens. "Yes."

"I am sure you have. She just bought all the artwork you left here the other day."

"The paintings you hated?" Vincent could not resist asking.

Rolling his eyes to the ceiling, Damien expresses a lambent sigh. Vince could feel the drama elocution over the fiber optic waves. "Yes."

A moment of silent elapses; thick acting, Vince could feel the bitch brewing in Damien slowly rising to the top like dead fish.

"Besides, one other thing, they bought out your contract."

Vince was not prepared. "What do you mean they bought out my contract? Do I not have a say in any of this?"

Vincent, you know the gallery has been struggling as of late. Frankly, it was a generous buyout. Nevertheless, Vincent, you should not have gone behind my back."

"Damien, you threw me out just like that? Wait a minute, your back? I didn't..."

Damien abruptly interrupts, "Vincent, you're going in a different direction. This is clear. Good for you. Do you know what the Dylan Welles Gallery gets for their artists' paintings? This is your long-awaited change. You're becoming a butterfly, my darling. Please, let us be kind to each other. I want to be remembered earnestly in your memoirs." Vince could feel it coming on, the love spat, scorned tone that Vincent overheard so many times at the gallery when Damien was wanting to scratch his partner's eyes out.

"So, when did it happen, Vince? How did that thin witchy snipe get to you? You know she has been trying to undermine me forever, as they say, to grow the rose of success, you have to nip a few buds..."

"Damien, it's not like that. I am not betraying you. This is just as much a surprise to me as it is to you."

Damien interjected with a cutting jibe. "Don't pretend you don't know. Well, my friend. You are about to find out. Stop in today. Some time, we will square all this out. I am keeping emotion out of it. Ciao."

Nicolette, tossing and turning in the next room, overheard some of the heated discussion. She calls out, "Vince, is everything ok?"

Vince starts laughing into the phone. He looks at himself from a hallway mirror. He runs into the bedroom and throws himself onto the bed in an exhausted thump. Rolling over, he grabs Nicolette and begins passionately kissing her neck and breasts, playfully undressing her quickly.

Nicolette, half laughing and half bleary-eyed, trying to recall why she was so angry last night, was now too curious to get angry; in fact, this newfound emotion in Vince was creating a new mind game, one she found difficult to argue with.

She quickly succumbed to his advances and in a matter of minutes, they were embroiled in a hot romp of passionate sex. It was not makeup sex, and it was not celebratory; it was something else, something new and different that neither one of them has experienced before; however unclear the motivation, the pure longing of passion that two people feel for each other permeated through each fiber of their being.

They kiss and whisper. With spoken breath, they make the invisible visible. Exhausted and expired by the ecstasy of human love, their bodies folded into the comfort of animal positions—a tigress rolled up and lion sprawled out.

"I have business with the Dylan Welles Gallery."

In a few hours, the sun was coming up. Vince lifted himself from the bed and ran for the shower. He began explaining things in part detail to Nicolette, who was tending to the baby who had just fallen asleep again. All is quiet except for Vincent's rambling.

Nicolette moves to the couch as Vincent's vague utterings fade behind the bathroom door.

The smile starts to fade from Nicolette's face as a blank melancholy look comes over her. She twists her hair. The sound of the shower pounded like rain.

Will I ever be happy? Nicolette thought to herself. She is listening to the good fortune of Vince and yet she somehow resents it. What kind of love is this that I secretly resent my lover's success? She thought to herself. Why am I not happy for him as I should be? Who is this child with us now? Nicolette's reasoning has become so obscured by the inflation and commotion of romance in both her career and her life with Vincent, that she is losing sight of who she is and what she does. "Tired all the time." She thought to herself. "Gaining weight."

In the middle of the night, Tramp the cat is drinking milk from an old wooden bowl on Mrs. McGivney's fire escape. He makes his way along the roof down a spout and into the alley. He meanders slowly along Jersey Avenue like a drunken sailor, past the taxis, nightclubs, and fast food vendors. Tramp turns on to a street, briskly trotting into a schoolyard. He passes three people huddled under an arched doorway, catching the echo of them singing Doo Wop oldies. One of them is drinking a beer from a brown paper bag.

The next few hours bring morning specials and newspaper deliveries. All The Way Ray blows a ring of cigar smoke from his newspaper stand while checking the racing results. Bright and early, the girls from the studio are checking in to rehearse.

Tramp hops to a ledge, jumps up, and makes his way to a window where he sits looking in at the dance troupe working out.

The mirrored walls and ceiling fans are keeping the girls thin as they scrutinize each move under the flourescent GE Light fixtures.

Ozzie brings her team to the front room to go over their tedious routines and work outstretches. The music is loud and exciting to watch. Tramp looks on through a closed greasy window.

As a climaxing crescendo builds to an end scene, Carla dances across the floor with a partner releasing into a full spin that launches her into a full roll and finishing halt.

The production of Ava is now in full swing.

Carla has acclimated into the troupe according to the needs of the business, and Ozzie is complacent with the new changes in the line. Any mention of Nicolette has now become just unfortunate folklore of a talent that might have been. Behind the scenes, Carla is diligent in keeping it that way, burying all current reports on her status.

Ozzie could not help thinking of what her friend Nicci is going through. She knows how much Nicci needs to dance. When they last spoke, Nicci was hinting to her about wanting to return to the studio; at best, it seemed a sad unreality. The performance waits for no one; Unless Nicci could fully commit, the show will go on the way it is planned. Although Nicolette is fine with every part of the lead, it would, however, require a herculean task to maneuver all the other obstacles.

There are two replacements available for secondary performers. Nicci could easily fill the part, but it has been months and Nicci is getting more depressed and despondent every day, binge eating and falling out of her routine. Mental prep alone is a monumental task. Ozzie knew in her heart, however, that Nicci, the real Nicci, could do it, but only Nicolette herself could make that happen.

The whistle blows; Silvestre the choreographer calls the girls to break. Ozzie falls out of line to catch Silvestre before he disappears.

Ozzie calls joyfully, "Hey Syl."

"Oz, what's up?"

"On the replacement for Edie and Kim, I know someone who wants to audition for the part. You Remember Nicolette Castro?"

Silvestre responds pushing a pencil behind his ear, "Nicolette. Ummm. Sort of, kind of," Silvestre answers with a slight puff of breath.

"Yeah, she was going to perform the part I have, before she had to leave, but now she is back and I told her I would talk her up to you."

Silvestre studies her from beneath an arched eyebrow, "You will have to speak with Marshal, Oz. He makes all the calls. You do know it's sort of a bible rule with him that once someone steps out of a part, especially in Nicolette's case, he would be hard-pressed to take them back. He hates excuses."

Ozzie cast lamenting cow eyes over Silvestre.

"I thought you could put in a good word, you know, a heads up, if it should come to you, that is."

"Ozzie, if I can help I will, but Marshal has the last word. I am just a flunky here too. You know how that goes."

"Understood. Thanks, Syl, you are a sweetheart."

Nicolette spent the day trying to put together the scattered pieces of a disturbing puzzle. Out of touch with the dance community, she felt like a lover missing her soulmate. It is reported that some medical patients who have lost a limb to accident or surgery sometimes experience a ghostly presence of the missing limb, Nicolette could not help herself from suffering the guilt of emotional detachment she was experiencing since her departure from the troupe.

That afternoon, determined not to give up, Nicolette asked Sonia to watch the baby. She took a walk along Marin Boulevard, where she slipped into the dance workshop and a separate entity from the studio. It was designed to help performers find opportunities and information that could be useful during trying times. The germ of an idea was forming on how to get back to dancing. Thoughts were churning in her mind for weeks. No one knew her plans, not even Vince.

A cork pegboard with job listings and business cards hung in the lobby of the workshop. Nicolette carefully studied the slips of paper and flyers pinned to it. She jotted numbers and websites, tore at makeshift flyers and notices, along with want ads.

For seconds, she was reminded of her early days as a dance student before she met Vince, the vigor and enthusiasm of finding auditions on her own, the freedom of rising and falling at your own expense, the excitement of competition. Those feelings were more important to her in those uncomplicated times than having a boyfriend; more significant than a contemporary life with a stable job and a house in the country as most girls her age would aspire to.

When she met Vince, it was his art spirit that drew her to him, the freedom to create that some men enjoy the luxury of more easily than women. She envied the sheer masculinity in manhood, the simple biological make-up of carrying a seed instead of a womb.

"Could two artistic people exist together?" she wondered. "Is true art more like a vocation or priesthood rather than a field of study?"

It is here in this subconscious part of me that God lives, a vision of perfection, a sense of wholeness and unity. He or she, whatever the entity may be, is part and parcel of that big emotional puzzle.

A man comes up behind her and excuses himself as he pins a flyer to the board.

It reads (DANCERS WANTED ALL STYLES IMMEDIATE PLACEMENT/ CALL (555-555-8726). Nicolette turns around and bumps into the man dropping her stuff. The man excuses himself and then notices that he has seen Nicolette before.

Have I seen you around here before? You are a dancer, aren't you?

"I worked here a while ago. I was away awhile"

Something about this man was familiar. Nicolette knows that she has seen him before.

"I hire some of the girls here; they work with us on their off-hours, earning some extra cash; some just to stay in shape or practice in front of an audience. Do you know Anna Thomas or Carla Davis from Ava?"

"Yes. I do."

Association with the name Carla Davis should have been a red flag. She thought, however, the temptation to see where this is going, was too enticing.

"Good dancers, Carla moved up, she made some money with us. It was a loss losing her to the theater."

This was not a theater person. She reasoned something vulgar and crude in his tone and manner.

"What exactly do you do, Mr. ahh...?"

"Sterns, Billy Sterns. I am the manager at the Galaxy over at Panama and Vine."

"The Galaxy...Oh, do you mean-ahh, Club Galaxy? That's a..."

Billy Sterns was quick to answer, "A gentlemen's club. Yes, exotic dancing, upscale clientele. No nudity. We only hire professional dancers. In many cases, a substantial source of income for some performers in between auditions. I like to think of it as a helping hand to community entertainers. Here, take my card, and ask for Billy. Tell them we spoke. It was a pleasure meeting you. How rude. I never got your name."

"Oh... Nicolette. Nicci Castro. Thanks."

They parted ways, Nicci holding the card, then putting it into her pocket.

Feeling mildly unctuous, Nicolette could not help detecting something of the pimp in his demeanor.

When coincidence is evil, characters have a way of coinciding to make drama for the Gods more pleasurable.

Carla Davis was on her way through the building for a completely unrelated reason; she ascended the staircase and entered the hall just in time to watch Nicolette talking with Billy Sterns.

She steps to the side and hides behind a wall not to be seen and observes them. Waiting for Billy to leave, she watches as Nicolette pins something to the board.

Carla walks over to the board and reads what Nicci posted.

She ripped it down and stashed it into her bag.

The apartment is a vapor pot of olive oil and garlic gently sautéing in the pan. A toss of fresh parsley covers a mound of golden linguini. Vince gently tosses the mix releasing a puff of fragrant steam from underneath the pasta. Floating some butter he sprinkles over it parmigiana cheese.

Working backward, Vince moves toward the table to clear it for the platted dishes before pouring the wine for dinner. Everything is ready for Nicolette when she comes home.

The table in their humble dining room section of the kitchen is always the place to stack: magazines, mail, notes, cameras, empty glasses, cell phones, and keys. These are the mark of modern apartment dwellers. Kitchen tables have been notorious dumping grounds from the first kitchen.

Rummaging through a pile of flyers, Vince can't help noticing some that were not usual junk mail.

Vincent, having made a pact with himself to support Nicci with her endeavors and support her, inquired little about her day without being too inquisitive.

"Nic, you were at the studio today. What is with the audition flyers? Any prospects?"

"Mostly amateur positions. I might have to start from square one; nothing on the level of Ava."

While shuffling papers around, Vincent notices a card fall to the floor.

He picks it up to read slowly; it is from the Galaxy club. He looks at it suspiciously.

"Oh, I wanted to talk to you about something," Nicci said, having noticed the card in Vince's hand.

"I was thinking of maybe working at the Galaxy for a while to kind of get in shape and get back into a practice routine, you know, until something comes through with an audition. What ayah think?"

"Nic, are you kidding me? You are asking me if I want the mother of my daughter to work at a strip club."

Nicolette, almost immediately defensive, covers the room with an air of disbelief, a tone that defied Vince's pseudo ignorance: his blind polarization to exotic dancing and stripping, the gray line between the two, the vernacular juggling of dance forms. Nicolette was not to be dissuaded.

"It's not a strip club, it's exotic dance. I could get back in shape; not to mention getting out of this cell for a while. Besides, the tips are good and this isn't about the baby, it's about me."

"Oh, I'm supposed to feel better about that, Nic. Are you forgetting you are a professional stage dancer? What you are talking about..."

"Look, Vince, I'm out of the loop. I have to get in shape, make connections, compete with girls that have less baggage than I do. I don't want to hang around here and playhouse all day. We're not married; you cannot make me not do it. Billy will help me."

Vince shakes his head and looks directly at Nicolette for the first time in the conversation. He is not exactly sure which subject to address first: the dancing as therapy issue or this new player that has just been introduced into the game, Billy.

"I am confused, Nic. You were the big baby advocate, remember? We had choices. I gave my heart and soul over to the one we made, no regrets. Where are you on this? I am sensing a role reversal. Who is this Billy character? I don't like him sneaking around, filling your head with all this bullshit. How long has he been coercing you?"

"Vince, you make it all sound so dirty. He is trying to help me get back on stage. He is not pressuring me to do anything. When I'm ready I can start any time I want. And leave anytime I want. He is a kind of life coach for people like me."

Vincent not feeling very comfortable with this is relying on a gut feeling that something evil is festering. Something disguised as an act of good intent, the primal instinct that a limping wildebeest might encounter while being circled by hyenas; the smiling hyenas bear no goodwill, they are not immediately threatening because they are small and are outnumbered by the wildebeest herd. The wildebeest, however, depends on loyalty from his herd to survive.

The lone wildebeest is always sacrificed by the herd, left behind to be devoured.

"And what is happening in the meantime while he is "counseling you?"

"Knock it off, Vince. Why are you making it sound so perverse? He is a nice guy helping me with my career."

Nicolette picks up her bag and walks toward the door. There was something telltale and animated in her body language, the actress playing out the next rehearsed scene in a script. It was a twist that led Vince to wonder if this scene was a psychological pulp or just something deep-rooted; unconscionably intended. He felt as though he was being led somewhere. It was unnatural like a room full of lights that cast no shadows.

"I'm going over my mother's for a while. I need to get some fresh air. Time to think. The smell of diapers is choking me. See you in a few…whatever."

It was strange. Her bag was already packed. It was that kind of thing.

Nicolette did not slam the door but did not close it gently.

Vince locked a puzzled stare at the door, then at the baby, who remained sleeping through the scuffle, adding another unnatural element to the episode. It is not clear to him who is wounded and who is abandoned.

Vince walks over to the table collecting some trash, clearing the neglected mess. Some stuff falls on the floor.

He begins picking it up and notices the lost letter from Lenny Paxton lodged behind the baseboard.

The first page was like a headline from a front-page story: Stark print and to the point.

He mumbles under his breath.

"Lenny is back early…son of a bitch, they were shooting at him"

The second page read: I am staying at the Brother's Hall for Jesuit Studies; Cell number: 555-2020.

The phone rings eerily; Vince picks it up.

It is a recorded message from the Dylan Welles Gallery.

"Hello. This is a special request for Vincent Galle; the Dylan Welles Gallery is having a dinner party at 350 West 52nd Street next Thursday on the 31st of October, 8:00 P.M. to celebrate Dylan's success at parker rounds. You will be receiving your invite card by mail with further details. Thank you."

Vince looks at the phone, then looks at the letter, and then looks at the door.

Brand spanking new Naugahyde stools of burgundy and gold line the bar like soldiers; course lighting accentuates the brass-plated rivets pushing dimples into the manmade fabric, adding a campy cheesiness to the decor. Expensive cologne permeated the stage. A very scantily clad girl called Brandi is dancing on a stage collecting tips from drinking patrons.

The music is boisterous. The crowd is a mixture of blue and white-collar workers drinking and catcalling the dancers.

Four Pakistani businessmen bicker over whose turn it is to tip the dancer as she sheepishly approached them.

The dancers knew the Pakistani businessmen were the worst tippers. Sugar Plum Baby told Lucky Louise, who passed the word to Brandi-54321 that you practically had to pry a dollar from them, and then they expected you to do every contortion in the Kama Sutra.

Tonight, one Raj was expected to pay the dollar and the other three would gather around him while she did her act. However, Raj did not want to fork over the dough, insisting he paid last time and left the tip for the taxi as well; while they were negotiating, the girl moved on to a burly trucker in town on a weekend layover. Without hesitating, he flipped her an Al Hamilton. The dancers loved American truckers.

The office of Billy Sterns was down the hall in the back away from the main floor. Usually, he sits quietly doing paperwork or napping. His window overlooks the street making it easier to see what's coming and going in the parking lot. He keeps a turkey sandwich in a small refrigerator and a bottle of cheap whiskey in the desk draw at all times.

Framed along the wall where most businessmen have reserved space for autographed signature photos of celebrities or certificates of achievements, Mr. Sterns displays showgirls. Judging from the style and discoloration of the photos, some of them would be so up in an age that they might now be paying a healthcare worker to watch over them.

Many of the dancers Billy had once employed have long since retired. Some have married up, but even hypergamy is a short-lived lifestyle in the skin game after the skin has become old and faded; long before that happens, however, their husbands are usually taken to the cleaners. There are whole beaches dedicated to these savvy women who live quite comfortably on their ex-husband's 401k plans, maxed-out credit cards, and investment properties.

Gently nodding after some phone calls and a bite from his sandwich, Billy was disturbed by a loud knock on his door. This door he usually keeps locked at all times, except for tonight.

From out of the lobby, Carla Davis bursts into his office accompanied by a huge ex-football player recently turned bouncer.

"I'm sorry, Mr. Sterns. She just got past me. I told her no visitors. You want me to throw her out?"

"It's ok, Ty. Miss Davis is more than welcome."

Carla turns to the security guard and addresses him putting on her best rudeness. "You hear that, Sparky?"

Ty the security person rich in tone as mahogany blushed with embarrassment, adding a somewhat noticeable tint of deep burgundy to his cheeks. He turns to exit and closes the door.

Billy sits back and studies Carla.

"Well, Carla, how you been?"

"Not as good as you, you mother jammin' double clutchin' jackass! I see you been raiding the Hen House again."

"You might have to explain. I don't quite understand the nature of this visit. Is something ruffling your feathers, chicken?"

"Don't give me that chicken shit. I got more important things on my plate than to be led down the primrose path of your malarkey; did you forget about our little secret already, our indiscretion as you call it? Do you think I am as easy to get rid of as…don't make me go there, Billy! Do not make me go there! This Nicolette you have been seen all over town with is just one more story."

"C'mon, Carla, it is business. She came to me for some work. What is your problem with her anyway? She is only trying to get back on her feet."

Carla has now slammed both hands down on Billy's desk. "Get back on her feet. Now you listen. I am not going to be upstaged by that skinny bitch, you hear me? The only help you had better be giving her is helping her step off."

The door opens, and Ty the security person looks in barely fitting his huge bald head between the door and frame.

"Is everything ok, Mr. Sterns?"

"Yes Ty, Thank you. Miss Davis was just leaving. Carla, you already got the part in that dumb ass play, didn't you? What are you still hanging around here for? We make choices in this world. Nicolette chose to have her baby. You aren't jealous, are you? On the other hand, maybe you are just having second thoughts."

Carla outraged, she exaggerated a gyrating head working the shimmy down her shoulders along her hips until it settled to the points of her shoes.

"Jealous! I'll show you who's jealous, you off the wall, son of a bitch. Maybe I should pay a little visit to Mrs. Sterns. You remember her, don't you? The one I have been playing second fiddle to, all this time. She is going to leave your dumb ass when I am done with her. And as for Nicolette, she will never work on that Ava Production or any other as long as I am around. She will rot on this damn stage right here, with the rest of these has-beens!"

Carla storms out of Billy's office, past Ty and some girls, who have gathered outside the door. Thirty seconds later, a loud screech from the street draws everyone's attention to the front of the building. People are running into the club saying there has been an accident; a woman was hit by a car.

Billy Sterns reaches into his drawer and pulls out the whiskey. He could have easily looked out his office window overlooking the street where all the commotion was generating from but chose not to. Instead, he walks over to the bar and sits himself up on one of those brand new spankin' sharp leatherette stools, leans against the bar, and calls over the bartender. He asks for a glass. The bartender brings a shot glass and pours from the bottle Billy had firmly planted in front of him. Billy asks him, "Hey man, let me ask you something. Do you want to do this forever?"

The bartender twenty-four years of age answers with stars in his eyes.

"I'm hoping one day to have a place like this of my own."

"How old are you now, right now?"

"I will be twenty-four sir."

"And you got into this business…Why?" Billy asked.

"I love to party and I love women…man this is the best job ever."

Billy smiled with almost a tear in his eye.

"Remember what I am telling you. Don't mix business with pleasure, and don't take on anything that your spirit cannot kill. Someone told me that once, but naturally, youth gets in the way of reality every time. Somewhere along the line, I have forgotten it."

Billy handed the keys to the bartender and told the security to lock up after Water-Mellon Rose completed her act.

He took the bottle back to his office, walked out through the back door leading to the parking lot, and drove away into the night.

## LENNY PAXTON

It has been four long months since Len Paxton has been out of the hospital. His bullet wound was healing nicely. He was happy on the occasions when Vince came to visit him. The tubes have been removed along with the stitches. He can walk almost completely upright again. Having grown a liking to the cane he was issued during recovery, he still carries it, not for its aid in supporting his walk but for the conspicuous fashion statement that a legitimate walking stick adds to his demure.

He has decided that it would be best to reinvent himself and move on, not be marginalized and corrupted by the absurdity and misfortune that brought about the loss Of Emily. What they had was unique. How they lived was a love story, but its time must now end.

Uncomfortable questions about injustice and divine providence entered his mind, so intense at times he was unable to concentrate on his surroundings. It was not easy philosophizing about God's actions. Has he been played for a fool? Why must he pray to scream, all the while hoping that life-shattering catastrophe is part of a bigger divine picture, something you must just believe in without any real attestation. The doctors said that the bullet just missed vital organs by fractions. Judging by the trajectory of the bullet, distance, and impact being taken into consideration, a twist or turn by the shooter in any direction by just a hair, would have been fatal. "Am I lucky?" or "Was I saved?" "What about Emily. And the horror she experienced as the last stream of blood poured from her throat after being brutally violated. Did she deserve that? Her last memory on earth is of senseless cruelty.

As an appointed man, am I to be judge and jury over God's choice? Will dismay, shock, and awe turn me to blasphemy? Lenny closed his mind unwilling to take that step, hoping the angel of prayer will cleanse his thoughts with gentle psalms.

He squeezed his cup of coffee; before him, is a copy of Journal Art News Magazine. Shifting his attention to the present, he looks over a full-length page advert presented by the Dylan Welles Gallery, along with an article featuring his good friend Vincent Galle.

The photos of Vincent's work were amazing, unusual, and with strange representations of modern life depicted in a setting of iconic medieval styles. Madonna icons are veiled in Versace spring clothes holding cell phones, baby angels hiding behind stylish eyewear. Gold flake and church glass settings are colorful, moving, and magical. Lenny was so mesmerized by the imagery and laurels of praise written about his friend that he did not hear Vincent taking a seat beside him. Vincent had the baby with him.

Lenny, moving from the Art Journal to seeing the baby for the first time, was slightly overwhelmed. His head is still foggy with the aftermath of burdening thoughts he blurted with surprise.

"Hey, Big Daddy. Look at you! So, this is what the stalk brought."

"How are you holding up, Lenny? You look better than you sounded in your letter. Much better since the last I saw you at the hospital."

Lenny putting on a false bravado responded in kind.

"It was just a flesh wound, every day, healing better. Maybe Sierra Narvon is not the right place for me after all. I guess they didn't like my guitar playing. How is our little angel?"

Lenny will be watching the baby; Vince needs to attend the Dylan Welles dinner party. Nicolette estranged in postpartum depression, soul searching in American style.

Lenny picks up the baby and starts to play with her.

"Don't worry, Vince. Do what you got to do. I'll watch her for you."

Vince jokingly reminds him, "Since you are slowly becoming the designated babysitter around here, Len, I might have to give you a crash course in diaper changing, not something that comes naturally to most men."

Lenny laughs, displaying a sly grin.

"I never told you about some of my training as a human services volunteer. Dude, I delivered babies in the rural villages of Haiti, watched over infants with diseases I can't even pronounce, and had to remove ticks from a starving 6-month-old. Believe me, she's in good hands."

Vincent's eyes drop suddenly. Lenny notices a slight tick in Vincent's smile is a twitch brought on by stress. Vincent confirms.

"I appreciate this, man. I don't know what's going on with Nicci. Postpartum depression, the doctor said. Mood swings, they come and go. She is staying at her mother's for a while."

"Go to the dinner party, Vince, everything is going to be ok. I'll be at your place by six. Just give it time. Nic is going through a lot. And so are you, this is a big break, this Dylan Welles thing. Looks like you could go international. That should cheer things up a little."

"You would think so, but Nicci is getting more resentful every day. It is almost like we are competing for success. I think she would be happy to see us both fail than to have me succeed and she never dances again. She has doubts about herself but encouragement is something she will not tolerate from me for some reason."

Both men order lunch from a cheerful waitress with big arms and a full waist. She prepares their table, a maternal type older woman who leans in toward the baby, her experienced eye in baby-rearing quickly caught on to the strange mix match, the color scheme of the child's clothes arrangement.

"Oh, how precious. Boy or girl?" she said almost mockingly, sending a note of pre-eminence to the young father in question.

"I'll bet Daddy dressed you this morning. You look like a little tomboy."

She adjusted the baby's green sweater that was loosely pulled over an N.Y Yankees tee shirt. The tiny socks were not frilly and the rest of the outfit served a basic function, lending not one indication to gender.

"It is customary that girls wear pink, even these days. Thank goodness that didn't change."

The woman spoke warmly. The maternity in her voice and natural love that glows in a matron smile unconsciously released a longing both men had missed for a long time. A memory triggered in Vince's mind of the time his first romantic advances were rejected by a young pretty brunette he had a crush on in grade school, and how his mother consoled him with advice and a glass of milk. When he asked his mother how she knew he was sad because of the brunette girl up the street, having never mentioned his feelings to anyone about the girl, strongly denying any concern whatsoever with the lass, she answered, "Do you ever get a feeling, Vincent, just before you sketch something, that it is just the right thing to draw at that particular time, that the picture needed it? That's called a hunch, and a hunch is creativity telling you to do something. Mothers have that all the time."

Lenny, at the same instance, could not stop the cascade of images of his mother standing over him when he fell from his skateboard bruising and scraping his knees; not being able to find a bandage large enough to cover the wound, she dressed it with a homemade gauze bind and scotch tape. However, it was the soothing tender love and caring that stopped the crying. That was the gift she left Lenny, an awareness of empathy and tender care that he carried in his heart, long after she passed on.

After the waitress turned and left, Vincent told Lenny.

"I love her, Len. I love this baby. I never thought that I could, but I do."

Later, the waitress returned with the bill. As they were leaving, the waitress was removing the plates from the table.

"She is just the cutest little thing. Daddy's little girl, I bet. There is a changing station in both restrooms if need be." After she spoke, Vincent became aware of the recognizable scent of a full diaper, slightly embarrassed that he had to have it called to his attention by the waitress; Vince looked up at Lenny and jokingly said.

"Are you ready for your first lesson?" they both laughed-a long-awaited laugh.


# DYLAN WELLES


On an exhausting day of mail, inspector Salvino Proust rests his head on his palm, sorting through the endless morass of inquiries from the media. His office assistant, a young intern, is answering phones and emails, putting people on hold and screening calls for him. The seemingly endless barrage of paperwork stacked on his desk is still mounting since the sudden death of Dylan Welles: international art dealer, jet setter, vogue superstar, and all-around bon vivant was found dead in her trendy New York gallery.

She was discovered by a custodian around seven-thirty in the morning, dangling from the scaffolding that was assembled the day before to install a piece of art from a newbie unknown artist named Vincent Galle. It was an apparent suicide, although no note or evidence thereof was left behind in New York.

Much to the dismay of the New York news people, she was found fully clothed, impeccably stylish in a Myron Kay Bach selection. Her raven hair fell back slightly angular in perspective to her head; a slight breeze from an overhead vent puffed a light arc of air between her neck and shoulders creating an unearthly animation to the stillness of demise. "A beauty's macabre," some papers wrote; others likened her to a hanging Venus Di Milo, "beautiful but not all there."

The only clue to what the circumstances were might be in the plastic envelope on Inspector Proust's desk, the few remains of pages from a personal book of poems that Dylan Welles left to burn in a fireplace during her brief stay in Milan. Inspector Proust had not turned them over yet to forensics; he had some time, time to think, time to feel. So powerful was this woman's "certain something" that even personal articles such as clothing and the paraphernalia related to her stirred fantasy and feelings of erotica in people. "Qualcosa di special."

Salvino Proust: His Father was Viennese. His mother was Sicilian. He was structured and masculine, a trait of Sicilians built close to the ground, and well portioned like his mother. However, there was an air of innocence about him; a fair coloring in his complexion that lent itself to his father's nearness to the Swiss Alps. His baby brown curly hair was whitening over the years, intensifying the cobalt blue eyes of his father. Although women have thrown themselves at him over the years, he had a hardwired innocence that kept him naïve. He was genuinely unaware of his good looks; he never took flirting seriously. He had a natural suspicious streak that always led him to seek out alternative motives in someone's sexual advances. As a police officer, he was thorough with facts; however, life in Italy has taught him that passions of the heart and mind can be powerful tools, dangerous to unskilled practitioners of "amore" who find themselves linked to games involving love and money. Drama is sweet candy for thrill-seekers. Dylan Welles was an American, different from European ways; perhaps not a conduit to evil herself, most likely a magnet.

Inspector Proust visited the Hotel Dylan Welles was staying at to speak with the concierge. It was strange that for three days, the celebrity art dealer had no visitors. The paparazzi knew nothing of her visit. In the celebrity news business, someone is always paid; information is always leaked. The concierge knew nothing. The bellhop that attended Ms. Welles's room was a dullard that was willing to swear Dylan Welles told him she was going to leap from the balcony after midnight. When later asked again about the story, he could not identify the correct room she was staying in or the clothes she was wearing the night he supposedly spoke with her. When shown photos of three different women, he failed to identify Dylan Welles as the woman he attended to that night, he chose the blonde actress from Norway. Back to square one.

Inspector Proust reclined on his broken-in sofa watching. Humphrey Bogart and Lauren Bacall banter back and forth in "the have and have not." He gently chuckled as he poured himself a Birra Amoretti, placing a sliver of thinly sliced mozzarella onto a cracker of toasted bread he gently covered with salted ham and tomato. Pushing it into his mouth, he sat back, pressing the volume button on the remote to make the television louder.

Since he was a young boy, Proust was fascinated with classic American detective stuff. His tiny apartment was filled with Noir novels and magazines he collected over the years; it was his only obsession. His favorite era was the American 1930's and 40's movies. He acquired items from mail order on fashion, art, and literature concerning the subject.

The cream yoke-colored walls of his apartment were stark and bare except for a 16 by 20 print photo of Lauren Bacall leaning against a post staring askew into the camera, her Veronica Lake hairstyle dipping below one eye causing a provocative cascading wave. He has four fedoras hanging on a door; two shades of gray, one black and deep green. The only other framed photos are of Bogie in his classic trench coat and Jesus holding a Glock 19, a muse cartoon cut from a comic book for shits and giggles. A chemical blue light halos from behind a pile of avalanching paperwork, research files, along with photos of Dylan Welles as she was last seen alive

A slim leather-bound notebook containing his recent journal entry lay open on a stool and it reads, "There is a little known history of Dylan Welles before her nineteenth year that is of any significant value. Her childhood is virtually nothing to speak of. Sarah Dylan

Welles as she was christened has only a childhood history of attending public grade schools. She lived with her aunt and her grandmother as "Sarah Welles" until their death and then she moved on. Her first known employment situation was with Temin Art Gallery N.Y. NY USA. It seems to be at this point, she began using Dylan Welles as her official nomenclature. Extended family? There seems to be no one."

*Note to self.* During her teenage years, there was no exact information available; a medical record indicates that on at least two instances, Sarah Welles was admitted to a local hospital for cuts around the arms and wrist area; minor cuts, however, symptomatic to what is referred to in American terms as cutting or slashing, cutting oneself with a knife or sharp object with the intent of self-injury. The doctor on staff who released the report was Eugene Gleason M.D./ Community health associates. It seems no psychological action was taken.

Current status on Eugene Gleason: long since deceased.

Vincent Galle pulls his motorcycle into the guest parking garage of Port Lux high-rise. The clicking of his shoes was creepy, reverberating in echoes across the concrete lot. The sinister characters inside the tiny security office, however, added to the eerie underworld ether even more so. Two unseemly persons who looked completely out of character in their security uniforms watched him as he made his way toward the exit. One of the security personnel stepped forward and called to him handing him a key card, informing him that he will need it to leave the lot. Vincent looked around; the TV eye of ominous security cameras watched over the sleeping Porsches and Audis.

The building was befitting to Dylan Welles. As he stepped outside looking toward the top, tracing the brick and light structure as it faded into a cloud of overcast October sky, one thing became clear to him: if there is such a myth as the Bohemian starving artist, the modern artist of today is being duped. The artists that worked in this environment were successful, not hauling heavy metal sculptures around or constructing frames and stretching canvas until their fingers' joints ached; they have assistants to do the dirty work. Most art schools never tell you that. There are ways to cut corners. Wealth does not always produce good art, but it is a clever business however that rules the day.

Vince began to feel insecure as he was walking toward the concierge desk. He felt like he was walking wrong. He became critically aware for the first time that he was walking like a working man.

It was Halloween; the concierge was allowed to wear one small item of decoration to acknowledge the event. This concierge was a tall and beautiful dark-skinned woman. Her name was Tatiana, according to her nameplate, her item of conspicuous opulence was a sparkling top hat with cat ears.

A group of giddy partygoers assembled in the lobby brushing past Vincent on their way to waiting cabs. Vincent took note of the full-grown men in costume and eccentric dressed women holding balloons and gift bags. Halloween was the one night people could expose their alter ego. It provided a license to be anything you want. What began as mild entertainment for children soon became a fantasy escapade for some adults, morphing almost undetected at times into the sexual realms of jackboot perversity and shiny leather.

Vince allowed his eyes to follow two witches through the glass revolving door. The lace on the second enchantress's short black skirt flared in the breeze catching between the door revolutions, pulling her skirt up over her thigh, thus exposing a bare buttock; with a tug, the woman of indiscernible age slowly freed the fabric from the door. Realizing she was putting on more than a show for this curious male stranger transfixed by her every move; she blew him a kiss before sashaying off to rejoin the group.

The rigor of circumstance that was infused in this place began to penetrate his senses; after a while, the effect of machismo in his walk did not seem to matter much in almost the same way Kurt Schwitters's collages of unlikely materials placed together and soon become complacent and pleasing to the eye once absorbed into the complete temporal landscape.

A humming whisper echoing through the room gently brought him back.

"Can I help you, sir?"

"Dylan Welles, dinner…ahh."

"Yes, your name, sir? And your invite card, please."

He looked up into her large brown languid eyes.

"Oh. Yes. Vince, Vincent Galle." He searched for the card and then handed it to the concierge. She checks his name on the list.

"Of course, Mr. Galle, take the elevator to the sixth floor."

Vince walks to the elevator then quickly turns back. "Excuse me. What is the room number?"

"Apartment number sir?"

"Yes. What door do I knock on?"

"It is the whole floor, there is only one door sir, and you will find it. I am sure floor six."

Vincent enters the elevator a little flushed, sheepishly waving to the concierge. Tatiana watches him enter, then picks up the phone, pressed some buttons, and then hits send.

"Mr. Lanier, Mr. Galle is on his way up. Yes, just now."

Three pings of the elevator and a swoosh opened the door and seconds later, Vincent Galle was staring down a long hallway stark and chrome gilded in an art deco design, on black lacquer tables, bunches of black roses, and white orchids filling the space. The original commercial art that was supplied by high-rise builders was replaced with original wall sculpture and high-end designer sconces. The only door to get in and out was being secured by a small framed figure coming toward him.

"Mr. Galle, you made it. Good timing, old boy. I am Basil Lanier, Dylan's project coordinator. How are things at the Sand Bar? Come in. I will introduce you to everyone. Dylan has been asking if you have arrived."

Basil takes Vincent's arm, escorting him down the hall.

"As time goes on, we will be seeing quite a bit of each other. You seem so tense. Relax. I will go over a few things with you."

Upon entering the room, Basil removed a small bell from his pocket. Ringing it, he stood silent in the room waiting to get everyone's notice.

"Can I have your attention please; everyone, attention. I am proud to introduce, the artist, Vincent Galle." With little interest, the guests looked on in silence.

"Follow me please."

Basil begins introducing Vincent to the other guests. Vincent is not listening; his head is spinning. The faces are just blending and distorting like a magic mirror at an amusement park. He looks up and out of the middle of the crowd to what appears to be Dylan Welles in a long tight dress with her black hair just falling all around holding a drink staring at him. How someone could envelop a cloak of isolation in a room full of people was the first spell that Vincent was suspended by. He shook someone's hand responding to some small talk. A sycophant lackey handing out business cards.

Vincent found himself scanning the room for the dark matron but she was gone. A large well-stocked bar in the corner of the room was lined with guests, no doubt wining, dining, and pocket lining. The whole thing felt odd. There did not seem to be any couples, just people milling around, no intimacy. Vincent could not help noticing a dwarfish peculiar little man with a cue ball head engaged in conversation with a large hefty obese woman. For her size, she was squeezed into a latex type of jumpsuit that was not complementing her many rolls of flesh and sagging skin. Vincent orders a bourbon and vermouth.

"Oh, a Manhattan, how quaint. Can we have a Manhattan here also, please? Bartender, shaken I presume."

Basil let out a giggle that did not quite fit the narration.

They settle back into their chairs and Basil takes the exchange.

"So, Vincent, have you met Dylan formerly? I suspect you have heard of her. She never joins the parties, one of her many little idiosyncrasies. She has been waiting to meet you. In fact, after your dinner, she wants me to bring you by. Is that all right with you?"

"Sure, of course."

Checking his watch, Basil rises from his seat.

"Good, now just make yourself at home and I will be making my rounds. If there is anything you need, just come and find me; have some hor's d oeuvres, and dinner will be soon."

Vincent is approached by a distinguished man brandishing a foreign accent; it was hard to tell what it was. It sounded Spanish, but could be French; his English, however, was like that of a Brit. He was speaking in several different accents.

"Hello. I am Franco. You are Vincent Galle, no doubt." After a cordial handshake, Franco continues:

"You are lucky the dinner party is on Halloween. There will be some amusing entertainment tonight. Usually, these parties could be dull. I entertain Dylan when she is in France, as they say; whatever Dylan wants. I am sort of an artist, in my own right."

Vincent not immediately catching on asks, "Oh, do you paint?"

Franco passed a markedly Mona Lisa half-smile, the kind that is best suited for the painting and always looks snarky on a man; he answered with a resounding, "No."

Vincent, feeling as though he was being led into an inside joke, started looking around the spacious entertainment room. It is not uncommon for people of celebrity and wealth to acquire whole floors in these luxury high rises and knock out the adjoining walls creating one large living space. It helped with privacy issues and allowed for more creative freeloading from wayward guests.

To the far off west end of the room, an area was roped off with velvet ropes, not unlike the kind you might see at a theater or nightclub. It sparked Vincent's curiosity and lent itself to an obvious entry into the conversation.

"Why is no one permitted past that room? "Vincent murmured dreamily. It seemed like a fair question.

A woman with an English accent was walking by protecting her Gin and tonic and chimed in, "That's her old auntie or something's room; she had it reproduced to exactly the way it was just after she passed on. Much of the furniture is the original. Had it transported stick by stick from the town where the elderly biddy lived. Been that way for the longest time. The dust is ye thick...a bit looney if you ask me."

"Rumor has it the old auntie still visits her now and then. She told me that herself. If you know what I mean." Excuse me, gents, I've got to make it to the loo."

There is loud laughter stemming from where some guests are gathered; an older man is drinking with some young girls. He is crawling around on the floor making mooing sounds, attempting to look up their dresses. Already completely drunk, he is obnoxiously crouched on all fours yelling to one young woman, "I am a cow, milk me, mooo. I am a cow, milk me." The man pretending to be a farm animal is the American artist Herbert Marcuse. Explained Franco, "He attained notoriety some years back for his painting on billboards of hyper-realistic porn scenes. He has since suffered a fall from grace having squandered a small fortune. Last heard, he is living off the charity of former art patrons who would rather have a has-been artist in their company than an unknown starving one."

Vincent turned to Franco asking, "Do you think that is true about the aunt?"

Waiting until the woman was out of earshot of hearing, Franco answered, "Of course not. It was her grandmother, I believe."

Revealing another snide smile, Franco turned from the bar, "Please excuse me. I see someone I must speak to before they get too drunk and forget me. I hope we get to talk after dinner. Adieu."

And hors d'oeuvre server took her place in the middle of the room ringing the bell again three times signaling that dinner was now being served. Not a word was spoken by the server.

The next event was something no one was quite ready for. A whistle blew as a wave of entertainment broke loose. All types of characters appeared out of nowhere, dressed as Charlie Chaplin to English beef eaters, jugglers, and clowns escorting the guests to their tables.

They served the food and poured the wine.

Amongst the merriment, a very beautiful mime court jester finds Vincent leaning against the bar and signals him to follow her. She leads him through a hallway to a room away from the dinner table and other guests. At the end of the hall, there is a heavy door. She opens the door gesturing him to go in.

Vincent finds himself staring down the length of a long beautifully decorated table. At the end of it stood Dylan Welles, all in black as before, except this time more enchanting. Candles are everywhere, and a fireplace is burning.

Vincent is disoriented, feeling the effect of bourbon on an empty stomach. He looks around at the walls. They are bare brick, with no paintings anywhere. A velvet curtain hangs off to the side. Just small cheap ceramic knick-knacks on an old antique table are the only room adornment.

When Dylan spoke, her voice was not anything like her physical appearance. It had a youthful pitch to it, somewhat like that of a little girl trying to sound grown-up.

"Hello, Mr. Galle. I thought we could dine in here. I hope you do not mind. We should formally introduce it. I am Dylan Welles. Can I call you Vincent?"

Vincent did not know what to make of it. This woman could not have been much older than him.

"Just don't call me late for dinner, as the joke goes." "Please be seated."

Servants begin bringing out all types of exotic food dishes tapas-style assorting them on the table: a champagne bucket is provided along with various bottles of wine. Music is pumped through the air. Another server starts sampling food onto Vincent and Dylan's plate.

"Buon appetite, Vincent."

Vincent was flabbergasted, to say the least. "This is quite a spread."

Dylan watched Vincent for a moment longer. "I have been told I have a vivacious appetite. As I presume, you do as well."

Vincent cleared his throat, "I try to count my calories."

"Basil tells me you are a chef as well as a fine artist. Maybe one morning, I will have the opportunity of having you cook breakfast for me."

Vincent just looks at her trying to remain cool.

Dylan gets up from the other end of the table and walks over to Vincent's side. He did not notice how sheer her dress was from the other side of the room; she had nothing on underneath it.

"Pour me some wine. Will you, Vincent?" Her voice seemed to have changed. Maybe it was the echo in the room or maybe something else. However, Vince was aware that Dylan can control it. Like the other facets of her life, her voice too was a tool for getting what she wants.

Vince removes the bottle of red vintage burgundy from the bucket and begins to pour slowly; the plunking sound of the wine hitting the sides of the glass was soothing and provocative. After the end of the pour, Dylan swirled the wine around in her glass.

Dylan holds the glass of wine up to Vincent as if to toast him then inspects the wine against the candlelight.

"Do you know what this is Vincent? Not quite vinegar, not quite grape juice, just wine. There are whole countries that dedicate life and prosperity to fermenting the grapes that rot for this very expensive stuff."

A bird flies through an open window way up the top of the cathedral ceiling, swooping across the room. Vincent flinched; Dylan hardly noticed her attention was focused on Vincent.

"When I was a little girl, I used to love grape juice, Concord grape juice. My auntie would serve me a cool refreshing glass with my lunch. Auntie would say, 'Sarah.' Sarah is what she called me, 'Juice is for children. Wine is for sophisticated ladies. Someday, you will taste the finest wine.'"

She went on, "When I first tasted the wine, I hated it. I thought about why they would take all the sweetness away. It made me feel sick. I was angry, about what they did to it."

Vincent listened intently.

"You know who puts the price tag on rotten grape juice and makes it more valuable than my beloved sweet nectar? People like me. Look around, Vincent. I am the most celebrated controversial art dealer of the time. I created markets all over the world from nothing. This is my apartment. I have no artwork anywhere in here."

Dylan moves over to stand by a window. The linear shade light coming in accentuates her nakedness through the sheer fabric of her dress.

There is nothing outside these walls, no piece of art the world would miss if people like me choose not to put it out there.

And in their naiveté, the creators of art would still paint more, knowing that people like me manipulate them every day. I cannot even draw a straight line. Any attempt to convey the images in my soul would be self-defeating. I see the world of nature as oppression, cruelty, and pain; as is the human world; but then again, I am not an artist. My emptiness is sleep, death, silence, and rest."

Vincent cuts to the chase.

"I am not sure if it's naiveté, for some people producing art is all they can do. If it is in you, it has to come out. Is this your poetic way of reminding me you can make me or break me?"

Dylan continues, "Concerning the wine, we soon come to realize that the first sip and the second bottle are indistinguishable to the palette."

Dylan slowly walks toward him. Her hair is now cascading over one shoulder. A bare cutaway in her dress exposes a long neck. Her hips silhouette in motion. Slinky movements contrast the burnt orange and blue dancing flames from the fireplace.

A thin bead of moisture began to break the surface just under Vincent's collar. Dylan reached down and unbuttoned his shirt. The invisible field of personal space has been violated. She lightly brushes his chest with her fingernails, rolling her eyes over Vincent's face, reflecting his own eyes like onyx gemstones. Her lips passed over the top of his right ear gently catching the fleshy lobe sucking it tenderly into her mouth; with his ear now held captive, she softly whispers on a vapor of thin breath.

"My part of the business is to swing the ax after the Bacchanal and Great expectations run their course. Nothing forever, you know. We are short-lived, you and I. So, let us start with the end. You can reunite with your conscience and your soul after the thrill of fantasy and crime diminish, providing you are wise enough to save a healthy portion of both conscience and soul for a rainy day. Sobriety at its best might serve well to remind you of your weaknesses or shortcomings, then my work is over."

Vincent, allowing his lips to brush across her throat, was still able to mumble as he spoke into the nape of her neck. Lambent kisses punctuated his words. "You have one hell of a pick-up line, D…"

Dylan contorts a sumptuous grin. She pushes Vince's head back pulling a frock of his hair gently. With her other hand, she holds the glass to his lips and pours wine into his mouth almost overflowing. He swallows. Slowly, his Adam's apple quivers. She raises her leg, resting her foot on the arm of the chair exposing her thigh, locking him in. She then pushes her breast into his face, holding the back of his neck, forcing his mouth back and forth between her partially exposed mounds, and staining her breast with wine.

Vincent stands lifting her to the table as her leg curls around his back, and they kiss passionately. Dylan's hands work their way inside Vincent's shirt, rubbing his chest. Her other leg comes up and catches around his back pushing her dress way up over her thighs. A shadow cast from the fireplace of two figures molten in coagulation of lust is a moving generated image, no faces or features, just the absence of light on two sinewy figures grasping and reaching. The dry heat of the fireplace brings with it a roasted whiff of cherry wood that mixes with the rising musk from Dylan's body. A delicate stream of spittle coated Vincent's quivering lip.

Three bells rang simultaneously as a call to order from the corner of the dark recessed room, surprising Vincent. His body shut down like a seized engine. Dylan hung her head back as a file of hair fanned across her shoulders. Through a blurry curtain of Dylan's frayed hair, Vincent could see a figure standing at the end of the long table, the clear outline of a male holding the little bell.

Making a staggering transition from ecstasy to an absurd arrangement in just a moment, Vincent was aware he was part of something more sinister than a spontaneous seduction. He felt the beads of sweat along his temple chilling quickly as a shock of surprise bolted through his veins. The man at the end of the table clicked on a small lamp over the mantle; a yellow tint lit his profile. Franco stood at table length searching the melted figures before him, studying the sultry spine of Dylan's back as it morphed into the strong line of her leg unraveling itself from around Vincent's ribs like a python.

Vincent, recognizing him from their brief encounter at the bar, "What the fuck is Franco doing here?" Vincent blurted out not quite knowing how to react.

Dylan untangles herself from Vincent and sits upright on the table like a cat, removing her earrings, studying Vincent. She casts a sideways glance at Franco, who is coolly looking on.

"This is where he comes in," Dylan said matter-of-factly. "You can stay, or you can leave now. I would prefer that you stay. Either way, I am still handling your paintings. What happens in this room stays in this room. That is the only stipulation."

She kisses her two fingertips and places them on his lips. "Now go if you are going. You are killing the moment. Happy Halloween…"

Vincent looks at them with mixed emotions as he adjusts his clothes. Then, he turns and walks out the door.

Dylan and Franco laugh quietly amongst themselves and continue laughing at the statement until he is way out of the room. Franco's Mona Lisa smirk branded an image into Vincent's frontal lobe.

Vincent, scratching his head, tucking in his shirt, and stumbling through the crowd, was feeling kind of stupid as he made his way to the door. In the hallway, he was waiting for the elevator feeling somewhat compromised and angry enough to storm back inside to break Franco's face then finish his fuck before leaving. Male aggression in check, but still at full throttle. The elevator door swings open, Vincent steps inside, and from out of nowhere, Basil Lanier blows past and squeezes into the elevator alongside him.

"We have to talk, Vincent. Do you mind?"

Vincent, still projecting anger, was not quite sure he was not going to punch Basil in the face. The diminutive stature of the man, in sync with his delicate posturing, however, inspired Vincent to rethink hitting him for no apparent reason; he might just throw him through the lobby window instead. Basil leads him to the lobby couch they sit.

"I did not get a chance to get back to you at the party. Dylan is very brilliant and rich. She was testing you to see what you are made of. She tries to seduce men or any artist male or female for that matter; it gives her a feeling of power for some reason or another. She will be handling your art but you probably will not be seeing much of her anymore. All transactions will go through me. Now, is there anything you would like to ask me?"

Vincent glares at him in a half pissed off, out-of-focus kind of way. He tries to make sense, struggling to remember this is their well-rehearsed game and he is the clumsy new player, the mark, the patsy. In simple childish questioning, he asks, "What does any of this have to do with art?"

Basil, in avuncular form, responds, "It matters to me only as far as my finder's fee and commission are concerned. You can do quite well here. So, can we look forward to working with you? Things could be moving very quickly from this point on."

"Ok."

"Is that a yes?"

Vincent, succumbing to Basil's unaffected logic and charm answered, "Yes."

Basil looks at his watch for the second time. "You will be receiving some paperwork from me this week with a check. Call at the number provided. I have to be back at the party. We will be in touch. I am so glad you came to the party, Vincent. I am looking forward to hearing from you. Do you need a ride or anything?"

"No, thank you. I feel I have just been taken on one. Just one more thing; who is Franco?"

Basil ponders the question with the look of someone who faithfully follows a sitcom on TV, but finds it difficult to tell you anything about it. They might know everything about the sitcom: every episode by heart but would hesitate to tell you the minutest detail if you ask about it.

It is Basil's own little secret as if he would lose the one upon you by way of sharing any unearned information; and then suddenly, out of the blue, when you think you are not going to get your answer, the informer will answer in full disclosure, spilling the facts of someone's life all over the table like a small change at a penny arcade.

Basil Lanier can do this with real-life scenarios.

"That's her husband, Franco Bernard Delacroix. Have you heard of him? Art forgery scandal a few years back, international ladies man, always involved in something but he never seems to get pinched. Nothing ever sticks. Lucky, I guess. He is up to something again, no doubt. He is also an international art dealer. Franco is staying here in the states for a while until a scandal blows over at one of his interests in France. Avoid him if possible. Good night, Vincent."

Basil goes to the elevator door. The lobby is filling up with people dressed for Halloween.

Mr. Irwin Marshal comfortably supports his sizable girth against the railing of the balcony. He puffs a cloud of smoke from his Churchill cigar into the direction of a huge ceiling fan hanging over the rehearsal floor of his pet endeavoring the Buzz Beat Dance Studio. Buzz Beat, he thought to himself, turning his head back and forth. What a juvenile name for a serious venue of the performing arts.

The new name was the bright idea of his investor and business partner's daughter who decided she wanted to be involved in theater production after her stint at NYU. With no one else willing to invest the capital needed to sustain the once prestigious Lowie–Aire Theater, Irwin Marshal took on the partnership of Craig Lawson and his silent partner Whitney Lawson, the newly graduated want-to-be producer. Fortunately for Marshal, through some shrewd Machiavellian contract loophole, Miss Whitney is mostly involved in name-only capacity allowing Marshal major control over the more creative goings-on in the house allowing things to move smoothly and make money.

Below, Silvestre and his assistance are rehearsing with the troupe.

Silvestre claps his hands, calling everyone to assemble before him for the announcement.

"Alright everybody, listen up. In light of Carla Davis' accident, we will be bringing in an understudy to fill in."

"What happened to her?" a redhead asked from the ranks.

"She was hit by a car. That's all we know."

"Who is the understudy? Why can't one of us do it?" someone asked.

"Because we need the body, and you guys are already there with your parts, and we can not spare you. I am not going over all this again. Now, c'mon, people. Cooperate. We have a lot of work to do."

A sculpted, lean, bronze girl from the back row added, "Ummm, ah, one of Miss Whitney's club friends no doubt, is comin' to slum with us for a while."

A gentle murmur of laughter and acknowledgment, disgruntled uneasiness, buzz into a hum of agreement.

"Now, now ladies. Let's not forget who is buttering our bread here. We…"

From above the balcony, Irwin Marshal cleared his throat at about half the roar of a mountain lion catching Silvestre's attention. He shot him a look; his right eyebrow arched, glaring at Silvestre. With some embarrassment, the red-faced choreographer returned to his talking points.

After some further briefing, the entrance door opens as the understudy comes in. She is late and unorganized, already breaking two rules before even introducing herself. She nonchalantly checks her cell phone and snaps her gum.

The troupe in rank and file just watches on with raised eyebrows.

One week later since the promise of the understudy first hits the floor of the Buzz Beat Studio, a frustrated Irwin Marshal looks over his black-framed glasses at Silvestre, demanding an immediate result.

"We have to do something. I have thirty–eight performers out there, and ten shows in five different theaters coming up very soon, as you know. And the understudy does not know the parts. What do we do?"

The lanky red-faced choreographer finds himself in an awkward position; he is the guy who has to tell Irwin Marshal the understudy for Carla has only one real qualification, that being; she hangs out with Whitney Lawson.

Beneath the illusory surface, the whole of the dance performance world has become a system of related and unrelated things, a sprawling network of bottom lines and balances equally subject to administration.

Marshal collects all the calm he can humanly muster. He leans forward, almost splitting his pants, spittling spews from his mouth in all directions as he speaks, "Let me answer for you, Syl."

"Good reason number one: I could not anticipate that Carla was going to be hit with a car, and the understudy is incapable of walking and chewing gum at the same time," He ranted on.

"Find someone very quickly or we will have to postpone these dates. Do you know what that means? It means if I have to get to good reason number two, I am not going to wait for reason number three to shit, can you?"

He throws papers down on the desk. Silvestre slowly backs out of the office.

Silvestre walks across the rehearsal floor; the girls are performing their parts; no one wants to look up.

He is looking around, pulling his glance over to the third formation.

"Ozzie! Step out here please and come with me."

Ozzie grimaces and steps out of formation, following in slow lockstep to the corner of the room.

"That girl we were talking about the other day, Nicolette, Perez, or Hernandez, what was it?"

"Castro."

"Yes. Do you think she can learn Carla's part?"

"I sure do."

"What makes you so sure?"

"Nicci taught and coached me my part. She was to perform Carla's part."

"Make sure you show up here tomorrow with her. You got it?"

As Silvestre is prancing away, he shouts back over his shoulder, "Watch out for lightning, ice, meteors, falling boulders, anything. And look both ways when crossing the street. I don't want any excuses, you comprendo?"

Ozzie, unable to contain herself, yells back in unbridled excitement, "You got it, sir!"


## LENNY PAXTON

Lenny fulfilled his duty as a nanny. All is quiet in the comfortable confines of Vincent's and Nicolette's apartment. With Vincent at the Welles' dinner party and Nicolette estranged at her mother's place, Lenny takes some time to think and regroup. He was playing his guitar again, playing soft melodies until the baby went to sleep, and then he began to write. The struggle was endless with each line bringing back a brutal memory.

The door opens. It is Vincent.

"Hey, man. I have to tell you. It sure is comforting to see you with a guitar. It reminds me of more simple times."

Vincent opens a bag and pulls out two beers. He hands one over to Lenny, who graciously accepts.

Still, in a contemplative state of mind, Lenny mentions, "When I was in Narvon, I was working on a rock opera with someone, an inspired piece. It was almost finished, then the shooting. Hell, mostly everything I owned, not much, was lost or thrown away. The music score lyrics everything, is probably blowing around the jungle somewhere. How was the dinner party?"

Vincent, caught by the abrupt turn in the conversation, not wanting to press the issue, answered, "The Dylan Welles gallery is going to represent me. And that's all I can say about it tonight."

Vincent was unable to talk about Dylan Welles. How he was so easily overcome by her seduction still rattled him. He had learned something about himself this night. He learned he could be taken by the right order of circumstances.

This is perhaps the only context in which command of one's senses loses its correct connotation. Tonight, on that table penetrating her like a beast; the order of gratification that Eros created for him was presented in a bacchanalia of flesh and temptation. He was driven to a state of vulnerability he was unaware of in himself.

Is it guilt he is feeling or the humility of being played so easily? Static triumphed over even mindfulness.

The scent of Dylan still on him, Vincent was becoming paranoid Lenny would find him out.

Vince takes a seat on the couch. He switches to a comfortable frame of mind, a place he can run to with his old friend Lenny.

"Hey, let's get that electric piano out of storage. We can pick it up tomorrow with the rest of your stuff. We could bring it back here. There is a studio in my future; you can compose there if you like."

Vincent, not waiting for a response, headed to the bathroom. He knew he must shower quickly before Lenny catches on. "My God," he thought to himself. "Would this have happened if Nicolette was here?"

He knew in his heart he would not have, but he convinced himself it was justified.

Early the next morning, Vincent and Lenny were walking up a staircase leading to the apartment where Len was staying. An elderly man is sweeping the hallway.

As Lenny unlocks the door, clicks and squeaks crack the silence of the dusty corridor. The apartment building itself was a former YMCA bought out by the city and refurbished, offering temporary housing to the indigent and homeless getting back on their feet. The apartments are small but comfortable, furnished with donated stuff from local charity organizations.

An old woman across the hall steps out of her apartment holding a sizeable box and hands it to Lenny. The woman said, "Excuse me, this came for you yesterday, Mr. Paxton. I took it in to be safe. I hope you don't mind. It might be important."

Lenny took it from her trembling feeble hands. "Thank you so much, Mrs. Kline. It was very thoughtful of you."

"No trouble at all; things are always disappearing," she said. The old woman possessed a youthful smile that recessed behind a wrinkled jowl.

They exchange niceties and the woman went back inside.

As the door pushed shut, a warm vapor of a potted stew escaped her apartment. Vincent called to mind how he missed preparing surprise suppers for Nicolette. One of her favorites was beef stew. Nonetheless, the sentimental journey did not last long. The dark fallout of Dylan Welles from the night before slowly began to superimpose on his pleasant reverie.

One body part at a time, the casted shadow of lust and profanity slowly soiled the sweet mental image Vincent brought forward of Nicolette.

In a second, he was exchanging cerebral dialogue once more with his dual selves, convincing himself how selfish Nicolette was for leaving, and how she brought this drama on herself.

The proverbial good angel of conscience looks on with the sadness of the world, helplessly, as Dylan's scarlet breast radiating like opal falls out from a flimsy blouse, artistically unfolding in Vincent's mind, while the dark angel of animus smiles with delight from the opposite shoulder.

Vincent watches Lenny's hand push the key into the lock. Only a moment ago, the simple mechanism of a lock being accessed by a key would have gone unnoticed, nothing more than just that, an ordinary function performed routinely every day; however, even the sound of a grinding bolt disengaging from the lock chamber stirs arousal of vulgarity throughout Vincent's loins. The demon Dylan is in him.

Lenny turns the key and enters the one-room flat. Some boxes are scattered around, two suitcases.

"I'll dismantle the piano. Those boxes are going. That is about it all the furniture stays. Good thing you rented that SUV. It will save us some trips."

Vincent picks up a box and moves it to the front of the room. They both start bringing cartons in and out.

A folder falls out from a box, some newspaper clippings, and articles about Lenny being beaten and shot. Included was an article about Emily's murder.

Vincent puts it back before Lenny could see him with it. Vince continues gathering stuff. Vincent notices a framed picture on the table of the same girl in the article.

Seizing a good opportunity for bringing it up, Vince opens the space for dialogue.

"Hey, who's the girl?"

Lenny stops what he is doing and just answers uncomfortably. "A woman I met in Sierra Narvon. She taught at the school."

"Is she anyone special? She looks like more than a friend."

Lenny reaches over, takes the picture, and puts it away. "Yeah, she was. I try not to think about that place anymore."

Vincent knew his old friend. He knew Lenny wanted to talk, but could not begin. Vincent hit a nerve when he opened up the subject.

"Why don't you tell me what happened there, Len? Who is Emily?"

Lenny looks up in surprise, almost anger.

"How did you know that name?"

"Ok, ok. I am sorry. I was not spying, something fell out of the box, a newspaper. I saw your name and I read it."

Lenny, catching himself dryly, responds, "I'm sorry, Vince. I didn't mean to snap like that." After a pause, Lenny sat down on a crate and recounted the story.

"Emily was wonderful. She was an English teacher at the school in the village; a missionary teacher from England. We became friends and then lovers. She was going to come back to the states with me. I loved her. She decided to stay on in that God-forsaken country doing God's work. I was happy to stay, as long as we were together." Lenny looked down, like a man losing his religion. "God's work. Is that how a charitable God rewards?"

Vincent is watching him listening.

"People are very poor there. Gangs of thieves gather around like leaves being tossed in a wind swirl. They nearly cut her head off. She was gentle and kind, always afraid to think about evil. I finally came to my senses a week later. My whole life changed. They told me a 10-year-old boy shot me. I found out about Emily in the news archives much later."

"I am sorry, Len."

They rummage through the apartment both pretending nothing just happened, alternately gathering stuff.


## Mom's place

Sonia checks her nails to make sure they are dry. She lifts a cracker from a dish and delicately places it into her mouth, being careful not to get any crumbs on her freshly applied lipstick. "I am going to a movie with Mom. Do you want to come with us? She is at the store. I am meeting her there, get dressed if you're coming. We are catching the matinee."

"No, thanks. I am going to hang here and read a book or something."

"Nicolette, how long are you going to be like this? Think of Vincent, think of the baby. They need you. You can't hang around here all day in your pajamas, making believe this isn't real."

Nicolette looks up at Sonia. "Sonia, you look so pretty, going out and all. You are so lucky all this shit did not happen to you."

Nicci went on, "I don't know. I just want to feel pretty again. Look at me. I am a wreck. I need to dance. I wish people would just take me more seriously." Nicolette looks like she is about to cry.

"We do baby, we do."

Sonia comes around over to the couch and hugs her.

"Vincent loves you. I know he does. Mommy says cruel and unusual things, but she doesn't mean it like that. She wants to help despite the things she says."

Nicolette explains, "The doctor calls it postpartum depression. It's not uncommon. You are going to be late for your movie. Mom's going to blame me. Don't worry. I'm working on it. I am."

"I know you're getting stronger every day. We will be back later tonight. I'll bring back ice cream, rum raisin, your favorite." They exchange smiles and hugs. "Why don't you call Vincent? He misses you so much. Even with Lenny helping, a baby needs its mother. My heart melts just seeing her. She is so beautiful."

Nicolette has been resentful of the baby and snaps when anyone brings her up. Sonia is aware that this bitterness could be part of the illness and lets it go; but still, in all, Sonia is struggling with the urge to grab her younger sister by the throat and smack her when she gets too bitchy.

Mother, nonetheless, has a harder time taking medical science seriously. When it comes to mothers and children, Mama believes that mothers have an intuitive edge over a doctor's advice. Needless to say, they are driving each other crazy.

Sonia leaves, slamming the door. Nicolette, glad she is finally gone, gets up to prepare a bubble bath.

She loves the bathroom in her mother's apartment with its spacious floor space and oversized old fixtures. The tub is big and roomy with plenty of cabinet space for all her stuff unlike the apartment she shares with Vincent where everything is marginally smaller and condensed for modern living.

While preparing the bath, she switched the station randomly on the television to a sports channel. It is a neutral distraction allowing her to hear the statistical chatter without having to focus on the subject and listen. With both mom and Sonia out of the house, she can relax and get into her head for at least a few hours.

Sitting in the tub, Nicolette scoops up a handful of bubbles and playfully blows them across the room. She picks up a hand mirror examining her face. The handle slips from her soapy fingers and drops to the floor. The soothing water and the soft murmur of the TV sports moderator droning from the living room lulled her into a catnap. She nodded gently as the warm water cooled around her body waking her.

When she later came out from the bath, Nicolette inspected her body in the full-length mirror attached to the door wondering why, in all her 24 years, she has never looked at herself naked with introspection before. After watching herself for hundreds of hours at the dance studio, practicing in her dance clothes, even during her pregnancy, she realized she has not scrutinized her body as a full-length nude.

She raised her foot to the edge of the tub and examined her calf; squeezing some gel from a tube, she lathered her leg and proceeded to shave the length of one calf and thigh then the other, slowly extending higher and higher, allowing the razor to glide to her genital area taking on a path of its own.

The blade, passing over the stubble parts, reminded her of how sensitive the skin is around the pubic zone and how course and nappy the hair growth had become.

She thought of Vincent and their last time together: the fighting and bickering, the internal longing, desperately wanting to be independent of him, all the while resisting the urge to be in love with him.

Rubbing gently, she applied more lather to the un-kept under bottom between her legs awakening a shiver from deep within. A pang of arousal rose inside her sending a quiver throughout her body. She dropped the razor to better command what she was doing. Her hand and fingers found their mark.

"And the players take the field," a sportscaster echoed from the TV in the other room followed by the standing cheer of a stadium crowd. "Right," she snickered to herself almost laughing at the irony, pretending to be masturbating in front of fifty-thousand spectators cheering her on.

The spasms she was inducing rocked her. They came on quicker than usual, weakening her knees. She reached for the support from an overhead curtain rod, steadying herself until the final wave ended, as the paroxysms subsided. Nicolette held sturdy, settling for a moment.

Still naked, she ran into the other room where her things were neatly kept in suitcases stacked in the corner.

She removed a garment bag from her make-shift dresser, unfastening a flimsy gold fabric bra and bikini bottom from their hanger, pairing them with a lacy white shawl that was Sonia's.

She watched herself in the reflection of the smudgy bedroom window, confused by her image. She danced to the music jingle coming from a TV commercial, a slow, sleep-walk, twisting grind, the devil waltz. Her mind drifts back to the day she was accepted into the dance troupe for Ava, a turning point in her life, the heat of rehearsals, struggling for accomplishment, her first meeting with Ozzie that spurned the friendship of a lifetime, and their plans and aspiring dreams of how they would one day break from these city streets.

A vivid montage of successful undertakings raced through her skull: she and Vincent making love for the first time on that pitch midnight rooftop, recalling how madly in love with him she was, or is?

The silly things they laughed about and how much she wanted this baby when she first learned of her pregnancy: ironically at first, it was an emotional rollercoaster to identify with Vincent's, not wanting the child's reaction. There was never any doubt from the beginning that all she ever wanted was to have Vincent's baby, emphatically because, and only because, it was his. She would have a piece of Vincent growing inside her. "Now it seems he loves the baby more than he loves me," taunts the voice from inside her head.

Still performing to the ghostly likeness in the glass, she whispers at her dreamlike reflection: "The very thing that should bind us is going to separate us."

The turning pages of montage images and distorted facts ran through her mind; it was flipped scripts and fantasy, unfolding at the speed of thought that hoicked desperate imagery through Nicolette's head. The hardest projection to slow down, however, was of herself, dancing at the prestigious dance studio with honor and acclaim, observing a jury of her peers in dream sequence applauding a stellar performance. The standing ovation grossly morphs into the hideous transformation of the surreal blinded by the cheap, cheesy setting of stage lights; leering men tossing dollar tips and drink invitations at her. The sentiment of compromise was weighing in and becoming overbearing.

The lewd laughing crescendo in her head became so loud she threw the costume away from her body, snatching her robe from the floor. Covering up tightly, she curled into a fetal position and began to cry.

After Vincent and Lenny finished the moving, they rested back at the apartment. Vincent was washing dishes and putting them away in between sips of beer. Men without women, watching TV and drinking beer, add in a measure of modern life like a crying baby, and you have the contemporary paradigm.

The emasculation of American men has been slowly eating a hole into the fabric of male culture for decades before it hit the tipping point. Vincent was doing the cooking and cleaning; Lenny, the whimsical boy, is playing the guitar with clutter around him, a child in the playpen; Tramp, the stray cat, nestled on the fire escape, freeloading and eavesdropping. Kings in their court are all content as clowns; even Tramp was soon belly up basking in the wholesome conclave of male camaraderie.

The next day, Nicolette is making her way to the train station. The demographic of commuters is a healthy mix of folks from all walks of life keeping it real, exciting just enough to get through every day. The element of danger looms with every passer-by keeping everyone on their toes with social graces at a minimum.

This is the first time Nicolette has been out of the house alone in weeks. She is still not herself, not enough to socialize, but if she does not get out of the apartment and away from Mother and sister, she will explode. That is what Nicolette tells herself. The real reason, however, was her appointment at the Galaxy. In secret, she had already made plans to meet Billy Sterns and take the job dancing until she could get back in shape and get back on her feet.

While on the bus in the aisle across from her, a little boy is staring at her.

A mother gets on with her young daughter who is wearing a pink ballerina outfit.

Some girls get on talking trash and listening to iTunes from a phone the size of a letter envelope. An ironic reference is that the icon of an envelope is quickly disappearing from the American frontier due to email. It occurred to Nicolette that she has never written a hand-written letter. Maybe she would write one to Vincent, contact him via "snail mail."

A tall, skinny kid wearing a baseball cap is just staring at his cell phone, skateboard under arm absorbed in tweet chatter. Everyone seems to have backpacks as though they are running away. The modern Hobo. People look at you so intensely when you are a stranger and alone.

The little schoolboy opposite her is staring again. His body small and innocent; nonetheless, his eyes are mature and curious. She could sense a man's eyes in the boy's skull; underneath, coveting.

Nicolette reaches the stop and gets off the train.

Street by street, she makes her way until she reaches the Galaxy Gentleman's Club. Two taxi drivers are idled, talking amongst themselves as Nicolette pauses to think. She is looking at the building's cold gray exterior, again, neon.

A few men gathered outside were dramatizing loud in an outdoor voice.

"Yes, it did. She came running out mad as hell. She didn't even look; that taxi slammed her."

The other man comes around holding a coffee, "For real? Lucky she ain't dead. Must be crazy. Drunk or sumthin."

The first man reports, "It wasn't the taxi driver's fault he couldn't see her come running out like that. She was probably drunk coming' out da Galaxy, long legs, pretty too…could's been doped up, who knows?"

Nicolette is aware of the conversation but not paying any attention to it; makes no connection to Carla. She just stares at the building trying to make up her mind.

Inside the Galaxy, Billy Sterns watches the clock. The wall clock was an advertisement prop given to him by a liquor salesman as a promotional. It was in the shape of a vodka bottle. The label was the clock face. He glances down at his schedule planner for present-day activities. Nicolette's name was on it. The yearly planner was a gift from Jamey Wine Distributors, LTD.

He opened the door looking past the cloudy room, to see if Nicolette was in yet, waiting somewhere. Nothing. He ducks back inside.

Strolling back over to the window in his office, he pulls a tattered curtain away. He notices Nicolette standing out there curbside. She is biting her lip looking around nervously.

Billy, on one hand, was hoping she would come in and take the job. As a business move, she would be a good draw. Nevertheless, he could not help being affected by her dignity and grace as she stood poised outside his club; he noticed the glare of chemical neon against the side of her face, imagining it as stage light, thinking how vulgar it would look with its sulfuric glow against her fine profile, how she outclassed it.

She would radiate under it from within. The tasteless stage spotlights would not be able to color her in pink and blue velvet as it did for the other girls, necessary to hide their flaws and peak the sensation of fantasy. Instead, basking her in a sordid shade would only diminish her appeal, possibly wilt her, until one day, her inner light would exhaust completely unable to light any longer. That would be a bad thing. Billy has seen it before.

She had something in her presence that was different from Carla or some of the others he took in. They wanted to be exploited. To control the primal instincts was their game, vanity being very much a part of them. Carla, for example, the dark angel who would much rather rule in hell than serve in heaven. She could manipulate; beating men at their own game, she enjoyed watching people fall in the grave hole they would dig for themselves, with the shovel she was all too willing to offer them.

Nicolette, on the other hand, wanted to excel. This place would eat her soul. He reasoned to himself. Billy Sterns has the power to determine this outcome. He had let things happen in the past that had eaten parts of his soul, along with so much of his body that was already being eaten away. He was recently diagnosed with advanced cancer; sporadic episodes of pain and blood were becoming issues more evident to him every day. He should do one good thing before he dies and not hire her.

A taxi driver noticed a distressed Nicolette looking over the damp, cold streets, and broken pavement. A carnival of chain drugstores and media centers.

"Do you need a ride, miss? This ain't no place to be hanging around. Are you lost?" the taxi man offers.

"No, thanks. I am waiting for someone."

"Ok." He rolls up the window and drives away.

Billy watches her through the window, and Nicolette turns and walks away. Billy just lets the curtain fall back.

Nicolette walked through every street from the train station to Vincent's apartment, a straight walk that could have taken the better part of ten minutes to a meandering two hours. Once at the apartment steps, the great chain of procrastination lingered a little longer.

The voices in the hallway made her stop. It was a woman alright and there was no mistaking the male reverb of Vincent exchanging a fond farewell. At first, she froze silent, ducking out of sight. When the in-house giggling got to be too much, she launched up the steps and was surprised to see Ozzie in the doorway with Vincent.

"Oh my God," Nicolette exclaimed from another dimension. "What is going on?"

Ozzie turned. "Nicolette! I have been looking all over for you. Are you ok? Listen, I have something to tell you. Nic, you are not going to believe what happened. I tried to call you, but the number is different. Oh my God. I thought something happened. No one has heard back from you."

"What is going on, Oz?"

Vincent chimes in, noticing tenants from across the hall, fish eyeing them through slightly open door cracks. "Girls, please. Let's go inside. We all have a lot of catching up to do."

Once inside, Vincent hands the baby to Lenny. Lenny is not sure what to do.

"Carla was hit by a car and has a broken hip. Silvestre sent me here with orders from Marshal to see if you are still interested in the part."

"Oh my God, Marshal! I thought he hated me."

"Well, he loves you now. I'm here to bring you tomorrow. Can you do it Nicci? Silvestre is freaking out."

Ozzie looks over to Lenny, who is watching her like a satyr, seeking converse from a handmaiden. Feeling compelled to explain, Ozzie directs her message to Lenny,

"Silvestre; that is our choreographer." Lenny smiles and nods like the village idiot caught in Esmeralda's stare.

"Oh my God, Oz. Well, I don't know with the baby and all, I…"

Lenny, without missing a beat, blurts out, "Nicci, I will watch the baby. Go."

Now, Vincent is scratching his head like the village idiot.

"Sure. I'll be here too, Nicci."

Vincent steps between everyone and engulfs Nicolette in a hug. Holding her tight, he offers a supportive look.

"There is some good news I have to fill you in on. A lot has been happening."

There is a knock at the door and some cluttering around as everyone stands silent. Nicolette turns the handle opening the door to be greeted by Mother and Sonia.

Mother, wide-eyed, responds in a flabbergasted response.

"Nicolette. Oh my God. What are you doing here?"

"I live here, Mamma."

"I know, I know. But you have been so crazy and stupid lately, I don't know how things are going. Vincent, how is the baby? Let me see her."

Sonia steps forward with some bags and hands them absentmindedly to Vincent while talking to Nicolette.

"We brought some things for Vincent and the baby. Mamma wanted to see the baby. Oh my God! You were so depressed, now you're here. I'm so glad. This is so crazy…"

"Sonia, you are not going to believe what happened."

"Oh my God. Tell me, tell me."

The girls are all talking at the same time; different conversations all going at once.

Vincent is watching all the chaos with a blank look on his face.

Tramp scratches and meows at the window. Lenny lets him in. Tramp runs through the house to escape an oncoming rain shower dampening the street.

The chaotic repartee continuous as Nicolette and Ozzie make plans to meet the next day.


Very early the next morning, in wee hours, Sonia and Mother are sleeping on the couch, and Lenny is at the table sleeping with his head in his arms. Nicolette is on the chair sleeping with the baby nestled between her legs and arms. The only card missing is the queen of diamonds; Ozzie left for home.

Vincent is wrapping things, preparing a backpack with picnic items: coffee cups and champagne. He tiptoes over to Nicci sleeping on the chair. His hands are full, backpack and blankets slung over his shoulder; gently awakening Nicci, he gestures to her to put the baby in the crib. Nicci slowly rises and lays the baby in the crib. Vincent signals her to follow him.

Vince and Nicci, tiptoeing, move through the hall and up a small flight of metal stairs that lead to the door securing the roof.

Nicco is giggling. "Vince, what are you doing? This is nuts."

"Shhh!" Vincent pushes the door open and steps out onto the roof.

Some pigeons scatter.

He spreads out the blanket and pulls a milk crate between them. He gestures at Nicolette to sit. He opens the backpack and unfolds some food: bagels, butter jelly, and coffee. The early morning is dark, but not too dark, with light coming up off the street. The soft combination of street light and tenement glare illuminates Nicolette like a Parisian postcard.

"This is where we would have our midnight dinners, Vincent. I thought you had forgotten."

"Maybe I did for a while, but seeing you walk through that door tonight made me feel like I did the first time I saw you."

Nicolette looked up from the light. "Things can go so crazy so quickly. In many ways, you know me better than I know myself. I am afraid, Vince. I am scared of letting my childishness go. Children have excuses for doing all the wrong things; it's hard to grow up."

Those last words lingered in Vincent's ears.

"Tonight, for as long as it lasts Nicci, you don't have to worry. Right now, no illusions, only what we have." Vincent walks over to a wall of high brick and fencing.

"When I was a kid, I used to love to go up on rooftops and pretend I was king of the jungle. As time went on and the things in my life got bigger and bigger, the jungle began to disappear as if life and all the bullshit became bigger than the jungle itself. One day, the jungle did not seem to matter anymore. That made me very sad. I don't want to know where the jungle is inside you, what deals you made, or what you feel you had to do to get back to that place for it to be real again. I just can't watch you get smaller and smaller. I can't let you disappear."

"Nothing happened, Vince, nothing that either one of us has to be ashamed of. It is just as you called it, illusions."

"Nicolette, you have to tell me that you love our daughter. All this, the gallery, the theater, they are jungles we want to explore, things we fancy ourselves in love with along the way. We cannot ever really own it. What matters is her, our child. She carries the egg, she brings life forward. My paintings, your dance, they explain things, but it's life that brings magic to the jungle."

They share glances; Vincent picks up the blanket and drapes it around Nicolette's shoulders. She pours coffee from the thermos into a cup and hands it to Vince. Nicolette snuggles up to him, and Vincent holds her. Nicolette whispers to him:

"I was afraid that you would come to resent me after a while. The wounds might not heal. In dancing, sometimes, the syncopation changes quickly. One and one becomes three. And suddenly, the entire math gets fuzzy."

They both begin to laugh.

"I'm home, this is where I belong. I could never be happy without you and our daughter. What do you say we go back and make breakfast for our family?"

"Let them sleep while we have some coffee. I can't move from this spot just yet."

Vincent was excited like a kid in a candy store. Dangling before him on a little metal ring was a key. The studio was a large vacant space in a retired factory that the Dylan Welles Gallery had a lease on for its warehousing and artist's needs. Vincent was to work there producing paintings for upcoming shows that would extend throughout Europe and the United States.

If ever a celebrity art dealer made the headlines glitter, it was Dylan Welles. Since her early start, she emerged on the scene in bangle bracelets from St. Mark's place to high heels from Europe.

From her humble beginnings as a desk clerk at one of the most renowned New York galleries, Dylan proved unrelentingly to be a quick study. She kept a file of all the top collectors and dealers from around the world, slowly winning their hearts and minds one by one, opening one tiny apartment gallery after another using the most prestigious addresses in the art scene and dropping the most important names.

Where does the start-up money come from to begin an endeavor so risky? Good business and lucky hands could bring you only so far in the art trade. Beginner's luck began to run out that fated day when Dylan was dealt with the Jack of Hearts.

Franco was married when he and Dylan first met, working on a divorce. Dylan was promoting an international show in Nice. Franco made a small fortune on international trade in foreign cars and luxury yachts, both of which were perfect vessels for moving illegal contraband around the world. When his shipments were first seized in international waters for illegal activity concerning the transport of poppy and arms, his direct involvement was lucrative allowing him to only give up his business interests, thus escaping jail time. It was then that he became interested in the film industry and high art. It was around that time that he met Dylan Welles, the fashion-chic princess of the metropolitan art scene. She was trendy and smart, needing lucrative cash. He needed someone who could move large pieces of art with sizable quantities of Iranian heroin concealed in the elaborate framing.

Dylan was smart and shrewd, but she never broke the law. If she was aware of his evil doings, she never let on; she truly loved the art business and built it up from nothing. She took artists off the streets and made them international celebrity icons overnight. To have your name brought up at one of her parties, even in a negative connotation, was better than being ignored by her; being ignored was a one-way ticket to extinction. Yes, she was the celebrity art dealer of her time.

Dylan and Franco had a quiet wedding in France and honeymooned off the Amalfi coast. Some say they were never really married, that she needed the publicity. However, whatever it was, it was not long before the slow corrosive nature of Franco's corrupt and perverse lifestyle slowly started eating away at the high chrome finish and precious metal luster of Dylan Welles' fragile veneer.

Dangling the key in front of Lenny, Vincent said, "I picked up the key to the studio this week from Basil. I'm going over to check things out. They said it should be ready. You want to come along?"

"I can't make it. I have a doctor's appointment downtown. Latest x-ray result, but I'll catch up with you later."

"Ok. See ya then."

From a crumpled piece of paper with scribbled directions on it, Vincent directs his vision to a turn-of-the-century brick warehouse half painted and sprinkled with graffiti. The recently installed large skylight windows reflect beams of the blistering afternoon sun.

Approaching the large metal doors, he let himself in. Once inside, the dull thump of hammers and construction tools led him into the direction of activity.

He takes the stairwell entrance and climbs to the second landing. In one of the rooms, people were stretching large canvases across the floor. The thick smell of rabbit glue pervaded the air; it is traditionally boiled, creating a gamey odor. Vincent felt at home. Metal tables and paint cans cluttered the rooms.

While captivated by the goings-on, a girl wrapped in a sheet scuttles past, slightly brushing him. He watched her go to a leather bag she kept in the hall and removed a pack of cigarettes. Glancing at him, she smiles, vaporizing down the hallway. He continues to the next room. Scanning the door number, Vincent recognizes it to be his room; the door is slightly ajar.

Vincent pushes it open.

Dylan Welles, Basil, and some unknown person in a frumpy suit with a beard are looking over some papers. Dylan sitting on a stool, dressed in her signature black dress, looked like a shadow against the whitewashed walls. Her red lips are the only color in the composition. Poised like a cat, her loose leg dangled to the floor. A suede shoe hung provocatively from her toes. They all notice each other uncomfortably; Basil calls Vincent into the room.

Dylan steps off to the side with the other man. She is noticing Vincent, staring him down from the corner of her dark eyes, not acknowledging him. Unable to stop himself, he directed more attention to Dylan than he wanted to.

Basil with usual charm and protocol rushed to the threshold to greet him.

"Vincent, we had no idea when to expect you."

"Vincent, this is going to be your studio space; you can begin moving your stuff in at any time. You will be sharing the floor with Casper Wyatt, he…"

Vincent and Basil turn to meet Casper, discovering he and Dylan are gone.

"Oh. Dear Casper and Dylan must be off discussing. Not to worry. You two are sure to be acquainted in due time. Nice fellow."

With Dylan and Casper Wyatt gone, there was not much for Basil to talk about. Finding small talk burdensome, Basil bowed out and made a quick exit after a few minutes of forced conversation.

Vincent, now suddenly left alone, begins to look around opening doors and examining closet space.

Next room over, he hears mumbling. The gurgling of the old water pipes added surreal dizziness to his mental clutter. He walked over to Wyatt's studio unable to resist seeking out Dylan. The door was ajar. The thoughts that ran through Vincent's head were a mixed hodgepodge of sordid images beginning and ending with what he might find behind the closed sinister door. Popping his head in, he was not prepared for what he saw.

All around the studio was a hoarder's collection of broken pieces of junk: boxes of screws and rusted tools, cases of vintage doorknobs, architectural salvage of all kind, mostly household and cellar items, ropes and pulleys, birdcages of different shapes and sizes, and wood, bamboo, or metal stacked to the ceiling. The insides of old television sets are ripped away from the housing like guts spilling out; these hung from the wall and ceiling. Mannequins and plaster figures tied with ropes were everywhere, sitting up in chairs and lying on tables in contorted poses, polymorphic shapes of foam, and rubber hung from rafters tied with elaborate knots. Knots so bizarrely intricate

Vincent wondered if they served a functional purpose in real life or were just manifestations of the artist's darkness.

On an easel, back out of sight, there is a painting in progress of a young woman tied with ropes in a strangulated position. Sketches on newsprint paper bent to the breeze of an old dusty industrial fan. The sketches and paintings all bore the likeness of the same woman. Space was cleared for a model to stand, with one spotlight hovered above a wooden pallet, the posing stage area.

Who are these people? Who is Dylan Welles? There was a door at the end of the studio, the soft horizontal glow from underneath caused a razor-like to slither line of light along the floor, invariantly singular and unbroken; it was disturbed only by the shadows of passing feet from the other side.

Vincent, aware of the creaking decrepit floor slats, did not dare to go any further. He slowly backed out from where he came, making his way back to the stairwell in a half stupor. Turning quickly, he exited hoping to be gone before meeting anyone else. His attempt was quickly thwarted by a woman sitting on the steps of the narrow stairwell landing, wrapped in a bedsheet, smoking a thinly rolled marijuana cigarette.

"Are you down the hall, second floor, room 2?" she asked.

"Yes," Vincent answered into a puff of smoke.

"I'm Hanna, an artist model. Do you use models in your work?"

"Sometimes."

"I am working with Casper. Next time you see me, I'll have a card," she kiddingly gestured to show she had no pockets. Her childish giggle disarmed Vincent, relaxing him somewhat.

Vincent recognized her as the girl in the painting he just saw a few moments ago.

"Ok. I just passed by his studio, you are the model for the painting he is working on, aren't you?"

"Yes, Venus in the rope I call it," she giggles.

"You mind if I smoke?" she teased.

"No, go right ahead."

She takes a puff with a casual nonchalance of the new norm, gently blowing the intoxicating smoke past Vince's head, slightly tilting her skull and pinching her lips, creating a smoke stream that wisped past his ear. Her eyes squinted just enough for a sparkle of hazel grey to escape.

"Nice meeting you. I got to get back. See ya around."

She starts up the steps. Her naked curves accentuated beneath the sheet with each movement. Hanna tugged at the sheet body cover, bringing the hem midway to her calf as to not trip on the stairs exposing the yellow purplish bruises around her ankles.

A few days have passed since the good news. Nicolette comes running up from the street. Ozzie is waiting outside in front of the building. They greet each other as Ozzie opens the door, and they both rush in. Standing before the rehearsal studio door, Nicolette steps back and takes a breath. Ozzie puts a reassuring hand on her shoulder. "It is going to be ok, Nic. You can do this better than anybody. It's the audition, and there will be plenty of time to prepare for the show. You are not alone. It's yours, take it."

The door pushes open. Nicolette is looking at Ozzie over her shoulder.

Silvestre is standing with a group of dancers and musicians looking over the music score.

Ozzie points him out to Nicolette. "If you need anything, I will be right outside this door. I am not leaving until you come back a winner."

Nicolette walked up to Silvestre, a tall serious man, new wave, old school beatnik in his countenance. Everyone stops what they are doing and looks up at the intruder; some recognize her and freeze still in their tracks.

Nicolette introduces herself, "Excuse me, Silvestre. I am Nicolette Castro. I have an appointment to meet with you."

"Yes, yes." He excuses himself from the others. "Miss Castro, please follow me." They sit on folding chairs facing each other in the chamber room of the big hollowed-out auditorium. "Ozzie told me you are familiar with this part. It is a miracle if you are."

Silvestre calls over to the group of co-performers, "Christine! Can you meet with us at the piano, please?"

Christine stops what she is doing and walks over to the piano; the piano is on the other side of the room. The studio is quiet, so the echoing of the footsteps is isolated and pronounced. Christine prepares.

"Are you familiar with the spring jubilee, Act 3 Scene 2?"

"Yes," answers Nicolette, joining a resounding echo from Christine.

"Christine! Play a few bars so Nicolette will know where we are at."

Christine proceeds to follow.

"Now we will take it from the top. Nicolette, you will perform it at this time, ok?"

Nicolette listened intently knowing exactly her cue.

Christine plays an introduction to the part. Nicolette waits for her entrance theme.

She is still in street clothes. Nicolette attempts to stand on her toes, realizing she still has her sneakers on and awkwardly tumbles, clumsily excusing herself. Nervously, she retreats to her gym bag to gather her dance shoes and awkwardly begins changing them before her jury.

Silvestre and Christine look on with condescending smiles mixed with impatience and a convenient eye roll. Nicolette stands trying not to twitch uneasily.

"Are you ready?"

"Yes," Nicolette proclaims through meditative eyes.

"Begin."

They went into it. From the first note, Nicolette took off like a cloud. All the right moves flowed to all the right body parts. The piano soared like a carnival. Nicolette was lifted above and beyond her natural boundaries. Whatever was taking her to this higher place, she knew it existed in her all the time but was never able to get to it as though a secret chamber opened up inside her releasing guardian angels.

She flowed and dipped touched heaven and came back to earth. Hell personified in a leap. She always had trouble mastering at practice, but at that very moment, the rise and hurdle flew through her like new-found magic. When the last vibrato of the piano note softened to a dull timbre, Nicolette remained poised like a statue that was brought to life for a moment and returned to marble with only a bead of sweat on its brow to indicate humanness.

Silvestre, transfixed, not wanting to show overconfidence, asked, "Can you do that with all the parts?"

"Pretty much. I may have to polish up a bit."

"Of course, not a problem. Mr. Marshal will be here in about an hour. Can you come back? He has to meet you before I can do anything."

"Yes. I will wait. Thank you."

"No, thank you, Miss Castro. That was magic. And thank you, Christine, and thank all of you in the Ava Dance Troupe. I love you. C'mon, girls. Let's get back to work." He blew a whistle and everyone scattered like ants attending to their various parts.

Ozzie signals to Nicolette, barely able to contain her excitement.

In exactly twenty-three minutes, the door bursts open. Marshal enters, coat flaring, swinging his briefcase. He walks past everyone in a huff, shared expressions of reverence on the performers' faces as he flashes by. He storms into his office and slams the door.

Silvestre gathers up his papers and takes a swig of his coffee. He looks at a clock on the wall and waits about 10 seconds, and then he walks over to Marshal's door, knocks, and then goes in.

Nicolette and Ozzie look at each other from across the room. They cross fingers.

Nicolette looks at the clock. It reads 9:45.

The next glance was at 10:00. The girls and other performers are long since working on their parts.

Ozzie walks over to Nicolette whispering, "Wow, they have been in there a while. We should already be into rehearsing. I hope everything is ok."

"It will be. Don't worry."

Across town at the supermarket, Mother is looking over her bifocals, scrutinizing the details of a holiday shopping list. She is leaned over the cart, her matron breasts hanging over the handle. She calls over to Sonia who is busy pulling a can from the shelf.

"So that's it! We are going to have Thanksgiving at my house. You tell your sister. I have the shopping list already."

"But Ma, you know Vince likes to cook. They might want to have it over their place. It's the first time with the new baby and all."

"Sonia, don't try to get out of it. We are having it, and you are going to help me with the cooking. Besides, you need the practice. What man is going to marry you the way you are?"

"What! Why do you have to say it like that? I know how to cook."

"You use adobe for everything. If you run out of sugar, you would use adobe. Besides, with them getting back together, Vince working day and night at that hell-hole Sand place, he needs the rest. Here, I made two lists. It will cut the shopping time. Take this one and go look at the Jamon, you know, the ham. I need some items over here, you go over there."

Sonia peruses the aisle with a basket in hand, picking at the various snacks, while Mother is leaning against her cart going through the veggies squeezing and smelling everything.

As Sonia reaches for an item, an elderly man of Latin persuasion is admiring her ample behind. He says something off-color to her in his native tongue. Sonia, understanding his antiquated crude dialect, admonishes him away.

The mother is busy searching for coupons from an overflowing envelope. Her unique filing system is a mystery, only Mother herself can understand it.

After some time at shopping, sniffing and squeezing fruits and vegetables, they settle at the buffet station. Loading their plates, they take a corner window seat and have lunch.

Outside the window, some men are hanging a billboard advert for the new musical Ava. Mother scrutinizes it suspiciously. How a woman can choose to dance over raising a family was a childish concept to her. What is wrong with her daughter's head? She thought to herself. And Vincent with those silly pictures he makes. These men hanging this sign have a bigger purpose than him. He should have learned to make letters for signs and paint them on cardboard. He would have a real job like these men, instead of drawing those silly cartoons that no one understands.

Lenny is unpacking his belongings that he and Vincent brought back from the mission apartment. There are books and clothes, along with some paperwork about his work at the mission. One of the items is a photo of him shaking hands with an elder from the school. Lenny regards the photo with a tinge of sadness. He stacks the remainder of his clothes in the suitcase he has been living out of for years.

The curious FedEx box his neighbor gave landed under his feet now getting kicked and shuffled until Lenny had enough of it.

He takes a small pocketknife from his trouser pocket and opens it. There is a note on the official paper on top of some wrapping. It reads:

> These personal effects were recovered near your residence
> at the schoolhouse in Sierra Narvon. We thought it best
> to return them to you.
>
> Sierra Narvon police authority.

Lenny begins removing some notebooks, papers, a hairbrush, and a mirror, along with a small jewelry box containing a leather bracelet with a mock wedding ring.

He dug deeper and pulled out a manuscript from a manila envelope containing the musical rock opera he thought was gone forever.

He then reaches down and holds up an object wrapped in brown paper, uncovering the cup that Emily kept in the shower stall with her name on it.

Vincent's first week at the new studio was a hectic nightmare. There was no activity from Casper Wyatt's studio. The only indication that someone used it for anything was the padlock on the heavy metal door. A few salutations from maintenance workers coming in and out to check on water valves and code standards were all the conversation Vincent had for most of the day. Vincent worked feverishly, stretching canvass and nailing frames together. He is hoisting up canvass, but he realizes he needs help to move some shelving and hold things in place.

He scans up and down the hallway and sees no one. Lenny is busy with the baby. He is on his own.

Resting for a moment, he looks out the window and notices a panhandler outside the building. He throws on his jacket and heads for the staircase.

The man, not far into his twenties, was unshaven and scruffy. He did not have the lethargic look of a drug or alcohol abuser but more like someone who might be down on his luck; in his back pocket was a folded want ad section of the local paper he was reading and a paperback version of The Razors Edge by Somerset Maugham.

Vincent approaches the man and negotiates a deal with him to come upstairs and help him. They make their way up the stairwell, Vincent explaining the work.

The man's name was Seth Larson, a transplant from Michigan to the East Coast looking for work, discovering quickly that life is sometimes different than it is in your dreams. Seth soon found himself homeless and working transient jobs. He was, however, quite handy with light carpentry work and had the muscle to help Vince get moved in. His studies in Literature and History were enough to keep Vincent intellectually stimulated enough to turn an otherwise tedious struggling day's work into one of light temporal achievement.

One of the first things Seth did after agreeing to the terms and conditions of the handshake agreement was to remove a small coffee machine and a bag of French roast from his gurney sack, along with small containers of cream, some plastic spoons, and disposable cups.

"Some things I found along the way," he quipped.

"God bless the child that has his own," Vincent added.

They laughed and told stories as the coffee brewed.

Nicolette is still waiting to go into Mr. Marshal's office. Seconds out of time, minutes out of mind. The clock on the wall now has moved 15 minutes. She momentarily closes her eyes when Silvestre taps her shoulder.

He is holding some papers in his hand and tells Nicolette, "Miss Castro, I am so sorry…" his voice, bringing with it a hesitation, causing Nicolette to sense a moment of rejection then to wince, "to have kept you waiting for so long. I mean, Marshal is on a conference call and is unable to see you right now. However, you can start this week with rehearsals, if you want. He has given me the ok." Silvestre holds out some papers and formalities for her to sign, which she did under trembling hands.

Ozzie jumps from the ranks, hugging Nicolette with tears running down both their faces. Silvestre, trying to show grace under pressure, manages not to get caught up in the emotional episode. Maintaining a professional poise, he claps his hands like a judge's mallet, getting everyone's attention.

"Ok, ok. Let's go, people. We have work to do. Nicolette, welcome aboard."

Nicolette turns, starting toward the exit. Ozzie retreats to the ranks.

Nicolette notices a get-well card for Carla Davis on the table, along with a donation box for a get-well gift.

Still unaware of all that has transpired behind the scene, Nicolette never once suspected Carla of trying to undermine her.

Nicolette innocently opens her purse, takes out some money, and puts it in the box. Then, she picks up a pen, and with the same trembling hand, she pens her name just under the get well soon citation.

So nice a night, a sickle moon cuts a slice like a penknife poking its blade through a curtained sky. Tramp is watching through the window of the Dylan Welles Gallery.

Vincent is directing the hanging of his paintings. Gallery assistants, along with Basil Lanier, are rushing around.

Maintenance personnel is preparing walls with whitewash and installing overhead lighting. A scaffold is being assembled in the middle of the floor. The pieces of a melancholy skeletal frame are heaped upon the floor waiting to be put together. Their purpose is to enshrine the main signature piece of the show. It is the artist's tribute, the large burlap coffee bag already hanging in the Sand Bar kitchen, a ready-made piece filled with broken plates with a single dollar bill pinned to it. It is a curious expression from the old man's demonstrative wit, showing his employees that the raises and stipends that they demand so frequently are being held hostage in the form of broken plates and wasted kitchen accessories due to their clumsiness and lack of regard for their employers' property and bottom line.

This object d' art is to be brought from the Sand Bar and reinstalled at the Dylan Welles Gallery by three o'clock in the afternoon. The movers were late, compounded with the scaffolding not yet up. The only hope is to have it halfway completed by early evening.

Little did anyone suspect that after its completion, the storm of notoriety the piece was about to receive would not generate its fanfare from any great leap of imagination, on behalf of either the artist or the parsimonious, penny-pinching Sand Bar proprietor, (the old man), but will come to owe its immortality to the stark black and white visage of Dylan Welles hanging from its rafters. Not only did she present herself in the most perfect style of dress for the morbid event, a vintage Coco Chanel pattern of simple vertical lines in black, navy blue, and white, apt to someone of her stature. No, it was the elaborate knot and lariat-style noose that caused the sensation. The texture of rope is silk-like hemp, soft like an expensive scarf, barely bruising the skin around her outstretched neck, the elaborate sequence of knots triangulating under the weight of her waif-like body, not your garden variety suicide by any means. This ritual was artfully considered and tastefully executed if such a thing is possible.

A stunning spectacle made the viewer wonder, is this still brutal death we are talking about, or is this a new form of high art? Could it be deemed a ceasing of existentialism, Chic Nihilism? This was what the art newspapers labeled it.

Repercussions from the European scandals concerning Dylan's operations and Franco's shady dealings were already rolling in. "Today's Mega opening of the Dylan Welles' biennial art show is already fraught with drama." One paper reported, "The glitzy dinner party affair drew celebrity collectors and art industry people from all over the world, dressed in velvet, gold lame, and fur." One prominent collector from Paris had paint thrown at her by an animal rights activist as she stepped from her limo to enter the gallery.

Besides negative publicity problems, the address was causing a stir.

The downtown location was not portraying "arty" Bohemia as some of the wealthy in-crowd; out-of-town patrons had thought it would, an exciting slumming adventure by some bored aristocrats quickly turned to an uncomfortable reality. There is true danger in the heart of the inner cities.

Graffiti artists were tagging cars, and although many undesirables were taken off the streets, panhandlers and thugs were still roaming around, making people uncomfortable.

Before long, there were several new lawsuits in the works. Art dealers were suing the Dylan Welles Gallery for damages. Claire Mayer, a prominent international dealer, presented the gallery with a lawsuit of two point five million dollars for series of paintings never delivered; she had purchased them from Casper Wyatt, C/O Dylan Welles Galleries. The negotiation was handled by Franco Bernard Delacroix. The paintings eventually turned up in an obscure warehouse in Senegal, packages of heroin with a combined street value of five million dollars were retrieved from the packaging crates.

Problems of forgeries and undelivered pieces continued to surface, and all seemed to be associated somehow with Franco's dealings. As more unforeseen lawsuits and scandals unfolded, Dylan was sure to be ruined. Franco was away in Europe unable to be reached.

The gallery is empty and dark. The only sound is the clicking of heels.

Perfectly manicured hand presses the light switch. On the other hand, she is holding a prepared noose of a special composition fabric the creation of bondage artist Casper Wyatt.

The room illuminates. Vincent Galle is the newest artist to join Dylan's stable of exciting painters. A beautiful full portrait of a modern Madonna on a cell phone unfolds looking down from a spacious heavenly partition. The large solemn eyes of the painting follow Dylan across the room almost weeping from behind large black-framed glasses.

A series of iconic paintings, Byzantine in their configuration, produced in gold flake and lead, envelope the walls. Contemporary mothers breastfeeding their overage cherub-like children while consuming sixty-four ounces of coffee lattés overflowing with cream.

A large mural of the Last Supper with homeless people on cell phones study her; Jesus is holding court on a computer answering emails, wearing an open hooded sweatshirt with a white shirt, and a preppy tie. Dylan smiles to herself thinking of the painting as a judge and jury of her peers. They hold the final verdict from an earthly world of systems that did not work for her.

The ambulance and coroners have barely left the scene.

Back at his apartment, Basil Lanier reclined in his study. He slipped off his Berluti bespoke shoes and massaged his toes. He scanned the papers before him and selected the one with the juiciest headline. He then turned to his computer and began to research each supposed fact with his inside information. He then picked up his cell phone and made phone calls to art brokers he was still in very good standing with.

Mel Varstodian was the man to see.

"Hello Mel, It is Basil Lanier checking in. I hope all is well with you. Oh, I am sorry to hear that. In light of things, I am moving in a new direction. I will soon be acquiring the entire Dylan Welles collections, as you know. Yes, Mel, I am handling the bulk of Vincent Galle's work as well. He is my sole prodigy...Ha Ha! You have been reading the papers. Can we make a deal?"

Meanwhile, Vincent's art prices continued to rise to record levels. Because of his direct association with Dylan Welles' alleged suicide, curiosity about his involvement with her made him a star overnight. Why was his art piece selected to stage the hanging? Was there a subliminal message behind it? What, if any, was his connection to Casper Wyatt?

Casper Wyatt, who in this deal is the joker, and the joker is wild. Casper Wyatt was becoming the main media target by way of his intimate involvement with Dylan and Franco Delacroix.

When the police questioned Wyatt at his studio, he sat back in an old upholstered chair with a powdery substance on his beard holding court with some friends. He offered wine and cheese to the detectives. At one point, he requested a joint to be evenly distributed amongst his guests. Marijuana being legal, the detectives were not amused.

Behind him was a framed antique poster chart depicting rope tying techniques, "knots for beginners." It highlighted a cartoon of an old salt-style fisherman handing a skein of rope to a young boy.

His model, Hanna, the young woman wrapped in designer sheets, sat cross-legged on the floor tattooed and slightly bruised around the ankles and wrists defiantly smoking a joint.

The workout room at the Dance Studio was humid like a laundry mat. Nicolette, stretching on the bar getting her poise back, a dull burn along with her hamstring muscle, brought back recollections and enthusiastic strength.

Ozzie is counting while Nicci produces a series of swift dance moves; sweat is beginning to form in droplets on the floor. A click timer goes off; Nicci changes position, ripping through sit-ups then crunches enough to make a Marine flinch. She breaks for a moment and then walks over to the carriage where her baby daughter is lying awake about to cry. Nicolette picks her up, pressing her against her bosom. She waltzes her around the studio in wide gaits to a Tchaikovsky ballet, part of her afternoon discipline, as baby floats comfortably into dreamland.

Back at the apartment, Lenny enjoys a moment of contemplation. With both Vincent and Nicolette away working at their craft, he can now resume piecing together the parts of a broken dream: the rock opera he and Emily began composing in the jungle of Sierra Narvon before their fated tragedy. The sweetness of knowing it will now be completed off-set, the melancholy of not sharing it with her.

It was at that moment the clarity of inventive thought came into his mind, that rare fleeting glimpse from another dimension, latent manifestations of a suppressed idea whose time had come to surface. It was triggered by something Emily had said to him on occasion, a chilly moment of uncertainty. He recently experienced the same sensation after looking into the eyes of Vincent and Nicolette's infant for the first time but was unable to process the message at that instance.

"In the circle of eternity, people come together from unrelated places sometimes, to complete stories that were written about them long before they were even born," Emily would sometimes say.

It was this cryptic phrase that made it clear to him that wherever he finds himself wandering due to the consequence of his own faulty inept decisions, whatever boulevard, road, place, or religion he clings to for a moment of internal rest, the story must be completed by God, the supreme wild card. With that being said, the invisible hand of fate that commands the quill must deem it necessary to deploy a simple weave in destiny to do so.

Divinity throws a saint into every dream. Wholeness of sanity and wits exist in that unexplained narrative that forces you to complete something, moving you forward, placing things in their right order, profound and effortless, at times ambiguous and baffling, or as simple and plain as a twist of fate. Just happening.

# PART THREE

It is Thanksgiving morning, slightly grey and slow-moving, with an ever so slight sliver of sunlight piercing the clouds; just enough to soften the frost on the rectangular city green.

Floats are being assembled for the Thanksgiving Day Parade. Workers are putting the final touches on street decorations. Objects are being hoisted and boards being painted. The Ava car float is near the presentation.

Drum and bugle corps are lining the streets. Drummers and horn players assemble in groups. Festivity is in the air; everyone young and old alike are feeling the magic of the change in season.

On the other side of town, outside the train station, by the newsstand, once again, Officer Nate Blakely has his hands full. A man playing his bagpipe refuses to be whisked away.

"Cmon, now. You can't be blasting that thing here. This is a place of business. You know better."

The man with a Scottish accent answers, "Jeez, officer. A man has got to practice somewhere. I got the parade coming up, you know. Give us a break. The folks don't mind."

The officer once again admonishes, "For cryin' out loud. Go to a golf course and see if they'll have ya."

Upstairs in Mother's apartment, Sonia reaches over and pulls down the window to keep out some of the street noise.

Sonia and Mother are prepping food and chopping veggies for the Thanksgiving dinner. Sonia rolls out dough for the pastelitos, little fruit turnovers, always the favorite of Sonia and Nicolette around the holidays. The old Cuban songs are playing on the CD player ranging from old drippy Boleros to Miguelito Valdes and Anselmo Sacasas. Mother waxes nostalgic over Sonia, toiling over her chores. Pulling up a chair, she watches her work.

"I knew this song well in my youth, Sonia."

"Yes! I remember Papa singing this when I was a little girl," replied Sonia.

Mother reached over to pinch some dough from the loaf.

"A sad truth about memories," she started, "is that there are only a few things worth remembering. Come here, put that down. I want to show you how to dance to this. No one does this dance anymore. You can be the one to teach it to your niece."

Mother and Sonia begin dancing around the kitchen, with Mother taking the lead. After they dance and laugh, Sonia sits by the window and opens it again. The heat from the oven is making the dining area mucho caliente. Sonia looks over at the table in the traditional setting. No adobe on the table. Picking up the paper, she fans herself cool.

Mother is putting the final touches on a dish.

The door opens and Vincent, Nicco, and Lenny holding the baby, all entries, are in a ruckus entry.

Mother is directing everyone to his or her seat. "Oh, Nicolette! You look so thin. Now everyone sits. You must be starving."

Sonia is still sitting in a chair by the window, fanning herself. Everyone is talking all at once. Nicolette takes the baby and puts her in the playpen. They sit to eat and start passing around the food, family-style.

There is a knock on the door. Vincent gets it. It is Ozzie. Lenny looks surprised but pleased by this serendipitous arrival.

Vince looks at Nicci. Nicci looks up at Lenny with a devilish smile, implying she knew Lenny would be pleased by Ozzie's arrival. Vincent is catching on to Nicolette's holiday matchmaking attempts. Nicolette stretched a board over two chairs forming a makeshift bench. Vincent pours the wine and they toast. Mother insists they say, "grace."

"And you two had better start going to church with that baby. I did not raise this family on luck, you know."

The morning papers are hitting the stands, headlines read: Ava Dance Musical Sells Out. Local Review: Dance Diva Nicolette Castro Wins the Night.

Two pages back in arts and leisure, a small paragraph in broad face type announces that the art world mourns the loss of Dylan Welles, more to come.

The next day was opening day for Vincent Galle's opening at "District Gallery," the hot new happening in Los Angeles. The gallery was recently seized and taken over by Basil Lanier in place of Dylan Welles' premature demise.

Basil wasted no time converting the built-in resources of a relic Hollywood social club the old (Palm coast) cabana that has long since been a hangout for the notorious and bored actors and actresses haunting the L.A. strip and turning it into a trendy happening; a place to be seen by anyone, for anyone who is anyone, in the new art scene he is about to create.

A theme bar and restaurant quickly franchised on the property to keep the patrons well feed and slightly lubricated at all times.

The California sun was setting in the west; back east, Dylan Welles lay covered up in a morgue sheet. Her pedicured toe was carefully tagged. It read, "Welles, Jessica Dylan: death from apparent asphyxiation and a broken neck."

Casper Wyatt was downtown being interrogated by local detectives; he hadn't had a drink.

One Italian inspector from Milan who no one seemed to know was carefully looking over the international artist's passport.

In Milan four thousand miles away, the magazine model Mia Atlanta is pacing her room waiting for Franco Delacroix to return. She has already been interrogated by chief inspector Salvino Proust and is beginning to get edgy.

Everyone is playing out their hand, except Basil Lanier, who is quietly holding a royal flush and is now silently filling the void left by the imploded Dylan Welles Empire before he throws his hand down.

Back at the coffee table, Nicolette shares a quiet moment with Lenny who is looking over a script.

"Vince tells me you are putting in some hours on your project. I am so glad to see you involved with your love of music again. Can you tell me anything yet, or is it still a big hush-hush?"

Lenny looks up from over his paperwork a little bleary. "Did you ever wonder, Nic, about that day when you had an interview with Marshal? Why Marshal kept you waiting so long? Why Silvestre had to come out to tell you about such an important thing, without Marshal?"

Nicolette studies the lines on his face for a moment before answering. "Mr. Marshal is an important man. He is making deals all the time. The fact that he was tied up was my good fortune. Who knows what questions he might have asked? He is not fond of performers with children, you know."

"So I have been told."

Lenny hands the copy of his rock opera to Nicolette.

*Peripeteia,* an Irwin Marshal production, written by Leonard Paxton. Genre: rock opera musical.

"I told Marshal to keep it from you and Vince. We were on a conference call together with some people when you auditioned. I purposely kept the details from you until all this other stuff settled."

"Details like what?"

"I want you and Ozzie to choreograph it, Vince to be the art director, and I will co-produce it along with Marshal."

"Does Vincent know?"

"He is about to find out."

"What about Ozzie?"

"That's what we were huddled over at Thanksgiving. It was not finished, but she loves the idea. You seem to be the only one out of the loop," he said sheepishly.

Legacy

Back at the apartment, it is a lovely afternoon in the city. Mother is babysitting. Sonia is in the kitchen, going through the baby bag that Nicolette left with her, sorting out the food and diapers.

Mother turns to look over at the baby that never seems to cry. The baby is watching her from the crib with big round Picasso eyes that see the world.

She strolls to the window and closes it shut. Returning to her chair, she drapes a blanket over their legs tilting her head back to rest.

The coffee pot begins to perk, "Thump, bubble, thump bubble, thump…"

Ignoring it, she stands once again moving over to the crib and picks up the baby.

"A long time ago, I held your mother in my arms just like this. So much to remember about those days. Time passes quickly and brings many changes, baby doll. I had a husband who would have been your grandfather. He smoked and drank and treated me like dirt. That is how it was with me in those days. I gritted my teeth and put up with it until the old man died. Nevertheless, we had a name. That is how it was in those days, Dolly, for better or for worse. We made a deal, and the bastard stuck to it. I'll give him that much."

She looks up at a picture on the wall of her dead husband.

"Till deaths do you part was what Padre Simonies said. And till deaths do your part is what it was. We called it a marriage in those days. It took place in a church, a holy sacrament, sanctioned by the most-high. Today, a judge on the TV program says it is cheaper to keep her. That is a saying that could only be popular in these times. An attorney replaces the priest, and Sacrament is a matter of opinion. I believe your grandfather loved his family. Although I have to admit sometimes, I thought the fear of God sending him to hell is what kept him on the straight and narrow."

Mother kisses the baby on the cheek and places her back in the crib.

Three months have passed.

The Omni San Francisco Hotel poolside is sweltering and lovely. Characters could not be more out of place than this east coast band of gypsies that flew in to stay with Vincent and Nicolette on their honeymoon.

Basil and Vincent are sitting at a café table poolside talking, while Lenny and Ozzie are swimming. Nicolette and Mother are playing with the baby at the kiddy pool. Sonia is fanning herself enjoying a champagne cocktail; her Maui floral dress and large straw hat provided the perfect cover for a sun-drenched California pool deck as she quietly sipped from her drink, eyes softly folding behind her large dark sunglasses. Sonia shared a predisposition to a natural tan due in part to her Latin ancestry, but she paled, however, in comparison to California sun worshippers.

"Would you like another drink, Miss?" A suave handsome server stood over her ready to take her order.

"Well, ummm, don't mind if I do," she responded.

She said something to him in her broken Cuban New Jersey dialect, and he answered back in what she perceived to be maybe Mexican. But still, they laughed and he brought her another frozen daiquiri.

At the Tiki bar, Basil sits back and lights a cigar. He puffs a cloud of smoke into the air resisting the urge to look at his watch.

He says to Vincent, "It's extraordinary how this all came to pass, Vince. I attended the funeral service. It was not much. Dylan had no affinity to any established religion that anyone knew of. Much of her family obscured over the years, and hardly anyone attended service."

"Franco couldn't make it? I am sure the authorities are put off that he was not there."

"It appears, Vincent, that our Franco Bernard Delacroix is on the lamb these days. His charges are still mounting in Europe. I do thank you, however, for inviting me to the wedding. I must say your wife made a stunning bride. Her endeavors as a dancer are an absolute success."